Cuffing Season

Monica McCallan

Books by the Author

Back in Your Arms
When I'm With You
The Flaw in Our Design
Then & Now
Tapping into Love
Perspective
Good Spin
Charm City
Back to the Start
Better than a Dream

The LadyLuck Startups Romance Series

Sweat Equity
Vesting Period

Synopsis

Maeve Murphy doesn't have much to celebrate this holiday season. Ten years ago, she moved from Kingsford with no intention of returning. But home came calling, in the form of her mother's unexpected death. The least thing Maeve wants is to make friends—she's only back in Kingsford to help her father keep the family business, Murph's, afloat.

Bianca Rossi, whose father is the chef at Murph's, moved to Kingsford four years ago from the hustle and bustle of New York City. She loves everything about the charming little river town, and her positive attitude and willingness to engage is usually reciprocated by the Kingsford locals.

Maeve's been resistant to Bianca's attempts to strike up a friendship so far, but a little holiday magic may be just the thing they need to push them both in the right direction.

Cuffing Season is a 65k full-length standalone novel set in the world of Back in Your Arms.

Cuffing Season

© 2021 By Monica McCallan. All Rights Reserved. First Edition: December 2021

This is a work of fiction. Names, characters, places, and incidents are the product of the author's imagination or are used fictitiously. Any resemblance to actual persons, living or dead, business establishments, events, or locales is entirely coincidental.

This book, or parts thereof, may not be reproduced in any form without permission.

eBooks are not transferable. They cannot be sold, shared, or given away as it is an infringement of the copyright of this work.

Please respect the rights of the author and do not file share.

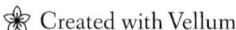 Created with Vellum

Chapter One

Bianca Rossi knew a few things about Maeve Murphy. She knew that Maeve hated when any of the regulars at the bar they both worked at, Murph's, referred to her with terms of endearment. She knew that Maeve loved the freshly baked bread served with all the pasta dishes. And, even though it had never come up between them, she knew that Maeve was conflicted about being back in Kingsford, New York.

But there were a lot of things that Bianca didn't know. She wasn't sure what Maeve's tattoo meant, the one that rested on her hip that Bianca would sometimes catch a glimpse of when the shorter woman had to reach for one of the liquor bottles on the top shelf. And she wasn't exactly sure why Maeve wasn't interested in making friends despite returning home more than six months ago to help her father. Or maybe she just didn't want to be Bianca's friend, which was... strange. Bianca prided herself on being kind and sociable with everyone she met and helpful whenever the chance presented itself.

It was why she'd agreed to pick up the Friday shift at Murph's, even though she worked full time as a receptionist at the veterinary clinic in town. Schlepping beer and getting hit on by tourists wasn't exactly her idea of a good time, but it helped her dad, who rented the kitchen out from the bar. His Casareccia cooking style was finally making a name for itself in the town, and she was proud to be part of it in some small way.

Another thing Bianca didn't know about Maeve was where she'd disappeared to. The kitchen had closed an hour ago, and her dad, Sal Rossi, had given her a kiss on the head ten minutes ago before heading home. Patrick Murphy, Maeve's dad and the owner of the bar, usually opened and then cut out after the dinner rush.1

Which meant that while Bianca could handle the customers who lingered on the Friday after Thanksgiving, finishing up their drinks after the last call, it wasn't ideal for Maeve to have wandered off.

She gave a quick nod to one of the regulars, Jeff, who scanned the room and gave her a quick nod back. Even if she didn't know where Maeve had disappeared to, she could at least start cleaning up so she wasn't here until two a.m. There were only about a dozen people left in the bar, and Jeff would keep an eye on things for a few minutes. Murph's was just that kind of place, one where people looked out for one another.

She grabbed the bag of trash she'd just tied off and headed down the long hallway to the back exit.

Late November was making itself known in a big way, and the winter chill hit her like a gut punch when she stepped out into the alleyway behind the bar.

In spite of the cold, she would have taken a few seconds to enjoy the flurries floating through the stillness of the night, but a ragged, breathy sound captured her attention. Her face flushed from the sound alone, but it was when she took a few steps toward the dumpster and the people beyond it came into view that her stomach swooped low.

Cuffing Season

Maeve had a woman Bianca didn't recognize pressed against the building's brick exterior, hands invisible under layers of clothing. Bianca would have been annoyed at Maeve's disappearing act if she wasn't so... intrigued?

Because this was another thing she hadn't known about Maeve: that she was interested in women.

"Oh," she said, louder than planned, her voice catching on the cold air she sucked in. Two sets of eyes tracked over to her as she stood dumbly with the trash bag still in her hand.

A curious half smile graced Maeve's usually stoic face, and she removed her hands from under the woman's sweater and shrugged before running her fingers through her mussed, blonde hair. Even from a few feet away, Bianca could see her wet lips.

Maeve didn't offer an explanation for what Bianca had just walked in on.

"I just... I was just taking out the trash. It's after last call, Maeve," Bianca said, willing her voice to stay even. Which was difficult. Her body seemed to think it was on a roller coaster, her stomach bottoming out.

Maeve smiled again at Bianca before looking apologetically toward the woman still leaning against the bricks. "I had fun," she said almost bashfully before adding, "you're good to get home, right? Do you want me to call you a car?"

Bianca knew surprise flickered across her face, but she tamped it down. So what if Maeve's dad owned the bar? Or that she was relatively nice to people she hooked up with in dimly lit alleys? It didn't give her a free pass to ditch her work and make out behind the building like a teenager.

Bianca didn't really want to see how long their goodbye would go on. She heaved the bag into the dumpster and shivered as the cold swept through her body. "I'll see you back inside."

Back behind the bar a minute later, Bianca started the process of closing out the remaining customers. Fleetingly, she wondered if Maeve would bring up what she'd walked in on outside.

* * *

Maeve allowed herself a few more indulgent seconds before sending—Betsy? Becca? Beth?—on her way. If she'd still been in New York City, this would have been a regular Friday night for her, sneaking to a deserted corner to make out with a woman she'd picked up at a party or a bar. She loved those first moments of connection, the tentative, teasing touches before things grew more intense. There was no drug quite as powerful as having a woman in your arms who wanted nothing more than to be exactly where she was.

Moving back to Kingsford at twenty-eight hadn't been ideal for Maeve's social life... or her sex life. It would have been easier, except she'd initially decided to stay with her dad since it was supposed to be a temporary situation. But two months had turned into three, and now three had turned into six. Getting her own place would be like admitting that she was staying, but continuing to live with her dad was seriously cramping her style.

And she didn't want to stay. She had a life in New York, and she had casual partners she could spend a night with whenever she wanted some company. Her old life hadn't given her much of a static schedule, so she'd kept things light, fitting people in when she had the time.

For the last five years, she'd worked as a junior photographer at a media agency, and just as she was starting to make inroads, life had gone off the rails. Her mom's death in a car

Cuffing Season

accident had upended the stability she thought she'd been building outside of Kingsford.

Suddenly, there were funeral arrangements and expectations placed on an only child to come home and do right by her family. She loved her mom, and it was her mom that she was doing these things for, not Patrick Murphy. He'd never understood her interest in photography. He'd never understood her desire to run off to the big city when there was a perfectly content small town filled with people who had known her since she was a baby to live in.

Maeve sighed and tucked her hair behind her ears, watching to make sure the woman she'd been with made it to the street safely. They hadn't exchanged numbers, but that was just fine with her. The fewer tethers she had to Kingsford, the easier it would be when her dad was in a good enough position that she could head back to the city.

If yesterday was any indication, there was no real reason for her to be in Kingsford anyway. Her dad had decided to keep the bar open on Thanksgiving, probably to stop them from any unnecessary and strained holiday celebrations without her mom around.

Halloween had been more about a revelatory party atmosphere, so it had been easy to push past that one, but the "family" holidays were fast approaching, and Thanksgiving had gone about how she'd expected, which was to say, it hadn't gone at all.

Sal Rossi was off with his family, Bianca included, so the only people who'd shown up at Murph's were true lovers of a cold drink in even colder weather. People with nowhere to go who didn't want to be alone.

So yeah, yesterday had fucked with her a little bit.

Which was how, after the cute woman made eyes at her for a while, Maeve found it easy to give in. To get caught up in something, however brief, that wasn't a painful reminder of her current existence.

Locking the back door behind her, she rolled her shoulders and braced for any type of conversation Bianca might try to have about what she'd seen. It was hard to pinpoint exactly what the look on Bianca's face was when she'd walked into the alley and interrupted Maeve's much-needed breather. Maybe a hint of disapproval that Maeve had shirked her responsibilities at the bar. That was deserved, but it was the other look, the slightly parted lips and sharp focus in Bianca's eyes, that Maeve couldn't get out of her mind. Bianca hadn't seemed offended or disgusted or judgmental.

No... she'd seemed a little bit turned on. And that had absolutely not been what Maeve was expecting when she'd heard the soft rasp of Bianca's voice interrupting the moment. Really, a voice like that should be illegal. It was husky and low and smooth like whiskey, and seemed so out of place on someone like Bianca. But somehow it worked.

It *definitely* worked for Maeve.

But if there was anyone who was on the *Do Not Touch* list, it was Bianca Rossi. Beautiful. Sweet. Helpful. She worked with animals for fuck's sake. Most importantly, their dads were business partners, and Maeve had no interest in throwing a wrench in the middle of the best thing that had happened to Murph's Bar in the last few decades.

So she'd intentionally kept Bianca at arm's length since returning to Kingsford, even though she knew it confused her.

Maeve had no intention of apologizing for living her life, but leaving Bianca to work the bar alone had been a shitty thing to do.

When Maeve entered the large room, a bar running down one side, with booths built along the opposite wall, she shot Jeff, the last person closing out their tab, a smile.

Cuffing Season

Jeff signed his receipt and rapped his knuckles against the polished bar. "You two have a good night."

"Night, Jeff," they said in unison.

After he left, Maeve walked to the front door and locked it. She picked up the cleaning supplies Bianca had placed on top of the bar and began wiping down the booths. "Thanks for covering for me earlier. Time got a little away from me."

"Yeah... um... no problem." Bianca wouldn't meet her stare. Interesting.

Beyond Maeve's own attraction, she hadn't let herself spend much time thinking about Bianca. Well, maybe that wasn't exactly true. She knew that Bianca had the prettiest, silkiest hair she'd ever seen. The kind of hair that would feel like running her fingers through water if she ever touched it. Bianca usually wore it in a high ponytail, and Maeve could get a little mesmerized by the loose waves that cascaded down her back and brushed back and forth along her shoulder blades when she was especially busy behind the bar or running orders. She knew from hearing Bianca talk to other customers that she worked during the week as a receptionist for the veterinarian in town and that she sometimes still cried when an animal had to be put down. Bianca had admitted that to Kelly Warren, one of her coworkers, when she'd stopped in for a drink one night.

Maeve had seen Kelly, her sister, Quinn McKinley, and Quinn's fiancée, Sawyer Kent, having dinner together in the bar a few times over the past six months. Thinking of them reminded her that it was probably her job to pass along news about special events to Bianca.

She braced her hands along the bar and shot a glance toward Bianca, who was prepping garnishes for the next day. Perfect, precise little slices of lemons and limes were cut with deft fingers and deposited gingerly into the tray slots. Everything Bianca seemed to do was a little bit perfect.

"Did Sal mention the special event two Fridays from now?" Sal Rossi made pasta that rivaled the best Italian restaurants in New York City, but if it wasn't about sauce or dough, he could be a little out of focus on details.

Bianca pulled her focus up from the cutting board. "That message did not reach me yet. What's the event?"

"Sawyer Kent and Quinn McKinley are having their engagement party here." So maybe it was also a chance to push the envelope she'd promised herself she'd stay away from just a smidge further.

The wide, bright smile that overtook Bianca's face made it seem like someone had turned on another light in the bar. She clasped her hands together and held them up to her chest. "That's fantastic news. I saw the rings last time they were in. I'm so happy for both of them."

"Me too," Maeve said sincerely. When she'd seen them in the restaurant together just a few weeks after she'd come back to town, it had been easy to wonder if something was going on between them.

She wasn't one for gushy, dramatic love stories, but when the two of them were around, the romance was almost palpable.

"Are they renting out the whole place?"

Maeve looked up to see Bianca's big, expressive eyes focused on her. She was the type of pretty that seemed unattainable to the average person. She'd taken down her hair, and it fell in loose, long waves across her shoulders and down her back. When she smiled, her whole face went along for the ride, her wide mouth and full lips broadening in a way that seemed so damn genuine it was hard not to smile right back.

Maeve ducked to hide her own smile and continued wiping down the bar. "They're going to be at the section in the back. We'll do a family-style menu. I think it's going to be about a dozen people. Nothing we shouldn't be able to handle together, even if we're busy."

Bianca nodded, absorbing the words. "They're really something to see together. At first glance it doesn't seem like they'd work, but they absolutely fit."

Maeve resisted rolling her eyes at the gooey sentiment. She'd had a sneaking suspicion Bianca was a little bit of a hopeless romantic, given how she always snuck glances at couples who seemed like they were on first dates. At first, Maeve had chalked it up to her own overactive imagination, but as the months rolled on, the pattern persisted.

Bianca wasn't overt about it, but she'd sneak a free dessert or spend a few extra minutes chatting the probable couple up to make sure conversation was flowing smoothly. Maeve wondered what the track record was for Friday night dates at Murph's, given the extra effort Bianca put into making them special.

When Maeve looked up again, an embarrassed smile flashed across Bianca's face. It was all of Maeve's time spent behind a camera lens that made her so good at picking out facial minutiae, what furrowed eyebrows or slightly parted lips or a soft gaze conveyed.

She'd spent more than a few shifts with Bianca, glancing at the cupid's bow of her lips and the clean line of her jaw, all in the service of capturing art and beauty. If not with a camera, at least with her memory.

"Did I do something to offend you?" Bianca looked at her with a soft stare, her fingers interwoven on top of the bar.

Maeve threw her rag behind the counter and started stacking the stools on top of the bar. "No?"

Bianca nodded, but only the memory of a smile ghosted across her lips. "Okay."

Someone like Bianca would either get eaten alive in a place like New York City or become the queen of it.

"I'm not really planning on staying in town much longer, so making friends seems a bit pointless."

"Oh," Bianca said before settling into quiet contemplation.

"But..." There was that frustrating need to fill the silence again. "I'm like this with everyone. I promise it's not just you. You've been nothing but welcoming since I've been back."

Maeve shook her head to clear the confusion. She really shouldn't have had that last shot an hour ago. It was making her tongue loose and her brain foggy. The woman she'd gone outside with had bought her one, but its effects seemed to persist after the taste of their kisses against the building were gone.

Bianca smiled more broadly again, like she'd worked out the answer to a puzzle. "Well, at least you're finding ways to enjoy the time you have left here."

With Bianca's stare trained on her, Maeve could barely remember what the woman from outside looked like. She hadn't had deep green eyes. And she definitely hadn't had a softness that made Maeve want to sink her fingers into her skin and pull her closer. Which felt strange to consider because Maeve had pulled the woman against her and lost herself in the sensation of lips and mingling breaths.

Maeve smirked to regain a sense of control and placed the last stool up on the bar. "A very glamorous life I lead. Living with my dad lends to some... creative problem-solving if I want to steal a few minutes."

She hadn't seen this look on Bianca's face before, one of amusement mingled with something else she couldn't quite place. "But your dad's okay with..." Bianca waved her hand, gesturing toward the hallway that led outside.

"Yes. He doesn't understand a photography career or a

Cuffing Season

desire to live in New York City, but weirdly, being a lesbian doesn't really ping on his radar for things to be annoyed about."

"That might be the first piece of information you've willingly told me about yourself."

Maeve laughed to cut through the truth of the statement. "Not here to make friends, remember?"

Bianca threw her bar towel over her shoulder and shut the lid on the garnish tray. "Seems kinda boring, but to each their own."

"Just stuck in a holding pattern right now, that's all."

With a nod, Bianca walked to the end of the bar and picked up the rag Maeve had used earlier. "I'm going to throw these in the laundry. Do you need anything else before I head out?"

"Nope. Thanks for your help tonight. And for, you know, covering for me while I was indisposed."

Bianca laughed and nodded, her eyes brighter again. "Sure thing."

It took about twenty more minutes for Maeve to close down the bar. She cleared the register and put the money in the safe, and she swept the floors and made sure everything was set up for her dad tomorrow.

At least with their work schedules, there were no pained family dinners to sit through every night without her mom.

As she locked up and headed out into the cold night air, she pulled her peacoat tighter around her body. The walk home was only a few minutes, but as she made her way along the route she took almost every night, she wondered what it would be like to have someone like Bianca Rossi as a friend.

Chapter Two

On Monday morning, Kelly Warren breezed into the veterinarian's office with an energy Bianca envied and placed a cup of coffee down on the reception table, sliding it toward her.

"If you keep bringing me coffee, I'm going to get used to it," Bianca said before taking a grateful sip. She was usually in the office for at least an hour before the vet techs and well on her way to wanting a second cup.

Kelly laughed. "It makes me feel less guilty if I buy one for someone else too. Let me throw my stuff in the staff room real quick."

Kelly disappeared down a short hallway. Bianca heard her steps quiet until she knew Kelly had wandered into the last door on the left, the staff room with lockers and a break room to hang out in between furry patients. As if there was ever a break between them.

Still, she loved her job. Dr. Anderson, the veterinarian, was great to work for, and Kelly and the other four vet techs were about the best coworkers she could ask for. Add in getting to see animals all day every day, and it was enough to make her want to work here until she retired.

The office was situated on a street a few blocks from the Hudson River, a little stand-alone, single-story building with white painted brick and a perfectly maintained exterior. The front door led to a seating area with enough room for any people and animals with an appointment, and Bianca's desk was part of a longer reception area that led to a hallway with the three exam rooms, Dr. Anderson's office, and a supply room. At the end of the hallway were two separate doors. One led to where animals were kept if they were scheduled for a surgery and the other led to the operating room where, thankfully, the most common reasons pets were there were minor surgeries and teeth cleanings.

Bianca had never gotten used to the hard stuff, even if she'd never let the pet owners see it. When she held someone's hand as they waited anxiously for news or accepted donations on behalf of a pet that had passed away, she always tried to make sure to remember that it wasn't about her. These people were fearful or grieving, and a little strength could go a long way.

Kelly burst back into the reception and waiting area, her own coffee in hand. Bianca smiled reflexively, pushing any thoughts about sick animals away. Leaning against the edge of the counter, Kelly looked over Bianca's shoulder at the day's schedule.

"Looks full."

Bianca expanded the view so the notes for each appointment were included. "Always, but we're busier than normal given the long holiday weekend. Luckily, though, today's mostly routine exams, and Dr. Anderson has a teeth extraction scheduled for this afternoon."

"No swallowed turkey bones requiring our attention?" Kelly asked, completely serious. It was a fair question because the year before, Mr. Porter had come in for that exact issue. His dog, ironically named Ham Bone, had gotten into leftovers on the Monday after Thanksgiving and thrown the entire day into chaos.

Who ate a turkey sandwich at eight a.m. anyway?

"If there was, we didn't get a call about it." Bianca confirmed the last scheduled appointments for the day and looked back up at Kelly. "How was your Thanksgiving?"

"Busy. With Sawyer and Quinn around this year, I decided to host at my house for everyone."

"But good, right?" Bianca studied Kelly, who fiddled absently with the brochures for various pet products situated at the edge of the counter.

"Absolutely," Kelly said with a bright smile before it dimmed slightly. "I mean, things with Quinn and my mom aren't exactly perfect still. There's some... lingering tension, but they're both working to move past it."

A few months ago, Kelly had briefly explained Quinn's conspicuous absence from Kingsford for so many years. It was difficult to understand Quinn's reticence about coming back without knowing why she'd left in the first place. It was hard for Bianca to imagine anything that would keep her away from her family for so long.

"Speaking of family events, I heard Quinn is having her engagement dinner at Murph's," she said to gently change the subject.

"I can't believe she didn't take me up on my offer to host it at the bowling alley," Kelly said with a wry grin, like she'd already let any thoughts of her lingering family tension go.

Bianca shrugged. "If it would make them happy to have it there, I'd be all for it. At least at Murph's, I'll get to bask in their love for a few hours."

"Right. I forgot you worked there on Fridays." Kelly looked

at Bianca a little harder, concern flashing across her face. "You're making enough here, right?"

"Oh, yeah. I mean, I'm not raking it in, but I make plenty to live on. Things were a little bit hectic when Patrick Murphy's wife passed away. I started helping out on Friday nights so that they didn't need to find someone new. Maeve, his daughter, took over most of the evening shifts for him, and there are a few other people who pick up shifts throughout the week."

Kelly seemed placated enough with her answer and nodded before taking a long drink of coffee and throwing her cup in the small trash can under the reception desk. "And how's Maeve doing?"

Even though Bianca had been the one to bring her up, even if it had been in a roundabout way, it still felt a little weird to talk about her. "I'm... I'm not sure," she settled on.

"I find that hard to believe," Kelly said with a laugh Bianca definitely didn't know how to take until Kelly added, "I'm pretty sure you know the life story of every person who's ever visited this office."

Kelly wasn't wrong, which made it feel even stranger to admit that she knew almost nothing about Maeve. Besides the fact that she liked to make out with women behind the bar, which was not something Bianca was planning to share.

"She mostly keeps to herself, and we only work together one night a week."

"You're around the same age. I figured you'd make fast friends."

"I'm probably as close to Maeve's age as she is to yours, Kelly. I love how you act like we're high school kids."

"Fair. I just meant that you're both young but also don't have kids. I feel like I'm thirty pushing fifty some days."

"Kids or not, I don't think Maeve has a lot of time. I think she works at the bar almost every night it's open."

Kelly's face grew somber. "I'm sure it's hard for her. She's really stepped up since her mom died. Patrick just hasn't been the same since."

Bianca had seen it too. Patrick, who used to be bright and exuberant and chatty, was a shadow of his former, larger-than-life caricature of a bar owner. His salt-and-pepper hair had gone almost completely gray in the last six months, and he walked like he was slogging through quicksand.

But when Bianca thought about it, there were things she knew about Maeve, the most important being: whatever Maeve lacked in communication skills, she made up for in action. That much was obvious. Maybe she wasn't trying to make friends, but she'd started working every night at the bar without a complaint as far as Bianca knew.

"Mmhmm," Bianca finally responded, lost in thought about how much Maeve must be going through, even if she wasn't showing it.

"Well, she can always talk to Quinn about picking up and leaving life in the big city."

These days, Bianca saw Sawyer and Quinn often. They'd stop by to see Kelly at work sometimes. They had dinner at Murph's once every few weeks. Quinn had just opened a real estate office downtown, so her business cards were scattered around local shops.

But until eight months ago, Quinn had been gone for a long time. The biggest difference was Kelly's excitement at her sister's return, at how often Quinn came up in conversation now. Before she'd come home, Bianca hadn't even known Kelly had a sister. "That's right. I'd forgotten about that. It feels like she's always lived here."

That earned a laugh from Kelly. "And against her best efforts, she found her way back to us. Though I'd have to credit that to Sawyer, mostly."

Bianca eased her forearms along her desk and put her face in her hands. "I love a good love story."

It was possible she'd watched every Hallmark holiday movie ever made, so she was thankful the new lineup had just started.

"It may take a few bottles of wine for them to give up the goods, but I swear I've never seen two people more made for one another. If anyone else decided to get married after five months of dating, I'd think they were crazy. But with those two..."

"It just seems right," Bianca finished.

"Yeah. Five months going on seventeen years. But I've gotta believe it all happened how it was meant to." She loved the sincere smile on Kelly's face, on anyone's face, really, when they were so truly happy about something that their body couldn't hide it.

A chill of excitement pushed its way down Bianca's spine. "I'll see how well I can casually pry at dinner next week."

Bianca's focus shifted to the door when it chimed, in time to see Mrs. Mulligan and her Great Dane, Scooter, walking through the front door. One of these days she'd really get a saddle for him, just to prove how much he looked like a small pony.

"Hi, Mrs. Mulligan," Kelly said with a wave before turning to Bianca. "I'll be ready in a few minutes and come back to get them."

Mrs. Mulligan waved back and moved over to a chair, cooing at Scooter to sit down next to her. Once they were both seated, they could look one another in the eyes.

With the first patient and owner, they were off to the races for the rest of the day. Even if Bianca loved her job, she couldn't stop thinking about her upcoming Friday shift at Murph's.

* * *

Maeve felt like she could handle a lot. Keeping odd hours to meet the needs of her photography clients. Living alone in New York City. Losing her mother.

Running around Kingsford in below-freezing weather was not on the ever-growing list of things she could handle. When winter had descended, she'd begrudgingly bought a membership to the local gym.

New York City hadn't seemed as cold. Maybe it was being enclosed in a concrete jungle, the heat from millions of bodies trapped together that kept a blanket of warmth draped across the city. It seemed, in retrospect, like the buildings blocked the wind off the same Hudson River a few blocks away, visible from the large window at the back of the gym.

That's how she found herself working out on a late Tuesday morning as she watched fat flurries float down to the pavement outside and melt.

Still, she was surprised at how much she'd grown to like working out here. She didn't see the after-work gym crowd much since she was always at the bar—except for Monday and Tuesday nights when Murph's wasn't open and she got a later start to her day.

When she was really ambitious, she'd work out with the retirement crowd early in the morning, running—literally—on a few hours of sleep after closing up the bar the night before. She loved their unnaturally dyed hair, like hitting seventy somehow made it completely normal to have purple-tinted locks. They'd gossip in little groups between reps at the lowest weights the machines offered, their morning routine as much for social engagement as fitness.

Sometimes, she thought about photographing them. Trying to capture the mundane acts that shaped their lives. How they always seemed to coordinate outfits and she wondered if it was something they discussed beforehand. They weren't the subject of her normal work.

In the city, she bounced among a variety of projects. About half of her work came from a creative agency, where she did whatever she could get her hands on: Branding photography for up-and-coming businesses and products. Some real estate photography, which included cringey headshots of all the agents and what may as well have been stock photos of their offices. She'd done a few advertising campaigns, but she'd hated learning all the contrivances that went into making something look better than it was. She wanted her pictures to be about bringing out something that was already there, instead of adding soap to a pint of beer to make it look like it had a fizzy head of never-ending foam.

The other half of her work was doing whatever someone would pay her to do—obviously within reason. Cheesy holiday headshots for a family of six in Queens: sure. Austere Christmas photos for a family of three on the Upper East Side: you betcha. She'd even been hired by parents to photograph sporting events to include in college athletic applications.

She could appreciate those photos for what they were, an accurate depiction of what she'd been commissioned to shoot. But they weren't the types of photos she looked back at in her portfolio. They were jobs that led to referrals for new jobs. At twenty-eight, she was still new enough that it would be idiotic to turn down an offer for work, even if the subject matter didn't make her feel anything except bored.

She realized she was doing it again and shook her head, forcing herself to focus on the high gym ceilings and the sounds of bodies working out to smooth rock that had never gone out of style with the current crowd. She couldn't keep thinking about a life she'd expressly told herself needed to be boxed away until she went back to New York City. If she didn't compartmentalize, she'd never make it through the day.

Instead, she centered herself on what was around her. It wasn't big by gym standards, but the main area had at least a dozen treadmills along with a dozen other workout bikes and ellipticals, and there were two rooms off to the side, one empty for yoga and boxing classes and another filled with spin bikes.

Still, she resented it, even if it wasn't the gym's fault. A membership was another tether, another notch solidifying her status as a Kingsford resident. She didn't want to be a Kingsford resident. All her mom had talked about growing up was her getting out of their small town and living her life. Meeting new people. Having big adventures.

It was hard to remember when those ideas had become her own, when she'd started to feel almost a physical itch on her skin to get out and see a bigger world than the one she'd found herself back in. Her mom must have seen something in her. Maybe it was how she'd always created elaborate stories for her dolls. Or maybe it was how she'd never had a whole lot to say to people, even if the gears were always turning a million miles an hour in her head.

She wiped a bead of sweat from her brow and bumped up her jog another mile per hour. It was ironic that it was her mother's death, of all things, that had brought her back here, stuck existing from day to day as she wondered what was next.

What if her dad didn't get better? What if he didn't find some way to exist in the new world they'd found themselves thrust into? With every step, she tried to focus on letting the anger dissolve from her body.

After the second mile, her breathing evened out. She moved closer to finding that meditative stride to let her thoughts clear.

Inhale.

Exhale.
Inhale.
Exhale.

    She breathed. And she tried to relax. And she let the metaphorical clouds float by. She did all the things she'd been trying to do every day for months.

    Christmas was coming up. It had always been her mom's favorite time of the year and the one time she made sure to come home. The irony struck again that she was already home, but it was unlikely that her mom's favorite holiday would be celebrated in any tangible way.

    Cranking her speed up another mile per hour, she settled into a longer stride that finally pulled her focus to anything except how lost she felt. Maybe if she ran fast enough, it would stop the thoughts from forming.

    Her legs burned. Her chest heaved with the steady, measured breaths she forced in. Whether she gulped or guzzled at the air around her, inhaling until she was dizzy, it didn't seem to matter. It couldn't fill up the emptiness she felt inside.

Chapter Three

"Mamma, please." Bianca pushed away her mother's attempt to put another serving of dinner on her plate. It was just the two of them on Wednesday night, her dad in the kitchen at Murph's.

If ignoring Bianca's protests was an Olympic sport, her mom would win gold. "You're too skinny."

She had Sofia Rossi's same green eyes, which were laser-focused on her at that moment. It was the one trait they shared, with all her other features coming from her father. Her height. Her long, lean body. Her dark hair, almost black and in contrast with her fair skin. With her features, she'd been mistaken for a native Sicilian more times than she could count growing up in Brooklyn.

Still, they'd been through this before. The life of a nosy Italian mother was never done. "Am not. You just watched me eat an insane amount of food. I'm built like Papa and Andrea and Franco."

She, her father, and her two older brothers had perfect builds to play soccer. Too bad they'd grown up in the United

States where the men's teams never stood a chance and training only started when they could walk, not when they were born. And too bad she'd been born with two left feet.

With a sigh, her mother returned the spoon to the pot. "I know you want to meet a nice man, Bianca."

"Person," Bianca automatically corrected before adding, "and all that would mean is more food for them. Provided we still cook enough for five people every night for dinner."

She loved when her mom threw her hands up in frustration, like she was doing now. Like words couldn't quite encompass her emotions. Both of Bianca's parents had been born in the United States, Bensonhurst to be exact, but her dad had retained his deep love for Italian cooking and her mom was the spitting image of her late nonna, whose hands always said far more than her broken English could.

Her mom switched gears. "You work too much."

"Everyone works too much. I don't live in the same world as you and Papa. Pensions don't really exist anymore. I'm trying to plan for my future."

"A lot of good his pension does with the havoc he wreaked on his body all those years."

"He was a good firefighter, Mamma. He helped a lot of people. And you were a great teacher. We still get mail forwarded from the old school from students updating you on their life."

That made her mom smile. "Don't try to butter me up. I hate that you work in that bar."

"And restaurant." Bianca rolled her eyes because they'd had this conversation more than a few times over the last five months. "I work there once a week to help out. Papa finally has the chance to follow his dreams. And he's serving Nonna Rossi's food. It's a wonderful thing, and I'm happy I can support it."

"It is wonderful, bambina, but I know you want other things as well."

So maybe it wasn't exactly a secret that Bianca yearned to find a love like her parents had. She had a job, two in fact, that she liked. She had friends she could call to hang out. And she had a family who adored her. But meeting someone to get lost in, to build a life with, had escaped her so far.

Bianca waved her fork around and ignored the sad feeling that washed over her. "You can't force these things, Mamma."

"You aren't helping yourself by working on Fridays. That's prime date night real estate."

That finally earned a laugh from Bianca. "I know, but it won't be forever. And people have different schedules all the time. You act like I live in a van in a national park or something and only come across humans once every three months when I trek into town for supplies."

"Your strange mind, bambina. You would have done great in my creative writing class."

"Maybe all those books you gave me growing up made me more than a little bit of the way I am. Have you ever thought of that?"

Her mom finally put the lid on the pot in the middle of the table and waved her off. "It was only supposed to be for a few weeks until Patrick's daughter came home. So why do you still need to work there?"

It was hard for Bianca to explain. She felt like she should be there. But explaining to her mom that she felt like she belonged in a bar wasn't going to be understood. "I like it. It's good for people watching. And like I said..."

"I know," her mom cut in. "You're helping your papa."

"And Patrick is a nice man. I feel horrible about what happened. I mean, could you imagine?" And what had happened to Maeve, too, but she didn't want to bring her into the conversation.

The look on her mom's face told her that, yes, she could imagine. There had been a number of close calls over the years when her dad was a firefighter.

Finally, her mom stood up from the table. "Just make sure you take time for yourself. Don't let life pass you by."

"I won't, Mamma."

Bianca didn't know exactly what she was waiting for. Maybe a sign. Maybe that flutter in the pit of her stomach when she locked eyes with someone across the bar. Maybe it was nothing more than a chance to soak in some community, something that had felt sorely lacking after her parents had moved to Kingsford and she'd stayed in New York City.

So yeah... she didn't know what she was waiting for, but she hoped she realized it when it happened.

Maeve never thought it would be Kingsford that made her soft, but here she was, getting ready for her Friday night shift and already tired to the bone.

Maybe it was the stress she'd felt this week. Nothing had really *changed*, but she'd had a restlessness, a feeling like she needed to start making decisions.

She'd stay through the New Year, but then it was time to head back to the city. If her dad didn't want to take responsibility for his life, she couldn't live it for him.

Back in her childhood bedroom, pushing thirty, caused a little twinge of something to well up in her. The first thing she'd done after coming back was removing the relics of her youth. Band posters. Drawings. Mementos of a kid who had dreamed of something bigger.

The only thing she'd kept was a photography book her mom had given her for her thirteenth birthday, beautiful images of people and places across the world.

Bianca would look right at home in a book like that. She pushed the thought away immediately. Of course Bianca would. Her dark hair and green eyes, with cheekbones that could cut glass, made it seem like she was formed in a lab somewhere. Beautiful was a relative term to a certain extent, but Bianca had the symmetry and facial structure that were almost universally agreed upon as *good*.

Thinking about Bianca was a long road to nowhere. She just had to make it through the next month. And tell her dad she was leaving. And make sure she still had work when she went back to New York City.

And while she did all of that, she didn't want to *feel* anything. Not lust. Not sadness. Not excitement.

All she wanted to do was get back *home* and prove to herself that the last eight months hadn't washed away ten years of progress.

If she had to ignore Bianca Rossi and the tenuous bridge they'd found last week, then so be it.

It was pretty clear that Maeve was back to ignoring her. That much was obvious as they moved around one another behind the bar on what had become a busy night.

The only time she came close to getting acknowledgement from Maeve was when, a minute ago, she'd slid a plate of pasta toward Patrick, who sat at the end of the bar. She'd put in the order for him around seven. He hadn't eaten yet, she knew, not because anyone had told her, but because his lost, faraway look was as real as the dark wooden bar her fingers rested atop.

When she walked away after a small smile from Patrick, Maeve brushed past her, voice low. "If you keep babying him, he's never going to learn to live again."

Her head whipped up and met the piercing blue of Maeve's eyes. Except they weren't bright. They were stormy, almost like she was angry with Bianca.

Bianca tried not to dwell on how strangely disappointed she was with Maeve's words, most of all because they were about her own father. "Everyone needs a little help sometimes."

Maeve slung a bar towel over her shoulder. "And some people get nothing but help."

Well, whatever that meant, it wasn't Bianca's problem. She smiled brightly. "I'm happy to cover the bar if you want to grab food too."

The darkness in Maeve's eyes was clearing, but Bianca wouldn't qualify the look on her face as *happy* by any stretch of the imagination. Still, Maeve's stance softened. "I'm good, thanks."

Suddenly, Bianca couldn't remember anymore why she'd had an anxious feeling of anticipation before her shift.

Maeve knew she'd acted like an asshole earlier. No one would ever accuse her of having an excessive amount of tact, but even she knew she'd crossed a line with Bianca, who'd just been trying to do something nice for her boss.

Standing behind the bar, Bianca was running through the closing process, humming quietly to herself. With her hair pulled up in a high ponytail away from her face, the green of her eyes became even more vibrant, and Maeve felt like she couldn't look anywhere else.

And more than that, she needed to apologize.

"I can feel you looking at me," Bianca said without shifting her stare away from the small dishwasher tucked under the bar.

Maeve cleared her throat, embarrassed at having been caught. Caught at what, well, she wasn't going to pick that apart with Bianca in such close proximity.

"I wanted to apologize. For earlier."

A soft smile pulled Bianca's lips wider. Bianca had a great everything, but her mouth was on another level. Sensuous was the best way to describe it. If she'd been anyone else, Maeve would have probably asked if she could photograph her, knowing a face like that and the effort Maeve would put into the shots would make it the anchor of her portfolio.

She fleetingly wondered what Bianca liked to do for fun, whether she ever went to Albany or New York City for a night out. Or maybe she liked to stay in. Bianca seemed... *intimate* was the word Maeve settled on.

Which was a weird word to pop into her head for a lot of reasons. First was that Maeve didn't much care about intimacy. Second was that she had no doubt Bianca could sidle up to almost anyone and leave the conversation with their information if she wanted. Maeve had watched more than a few guys slip their numbers to her across the bar before leaving.

It was, however unfounded, just a *feeling* that Maeve had.

God, the holidays were making her sentimental. People had had their homes decked out with garish decorations since Thanksgiving, and it felt like everywhere she turned, she was inundated with families and tidings of joy and togetherness.

But more importantly, and what she should have been focusing on, was the fact that Bianca was probably a settle-and-nest type, which only reinforced that she shouldn't let her fantasy run wild.

Still, it was difficult when Bianca looked at her the way she was now, her lush, lower lip pulled between her teeth.

Maeve found the strength to shake the visual out of her mind, even if Bianca was still standing in front of her looking like that after a six-hour shift and probably a full day at the veterinarian's office.

"So is that a no on accepting my apology?" Maeve asked with a slight shrug, pretending that the answer didn't really bother her one way or another.

It seemed, though, that if you did something damning enough to warrant Bianca Rossi not liking you—because she liked everyone—hell was your only possible destination.

Biana let go of her lip and ran her tongue across it soothingly before speaking. "I would accept your apology, but you have nothing to apologize for."

Heaven should just open up and take Bianca back to where she belonged. It wasn't down here on Earth with the mortals.

Maeve would have laughed at the absurdity of the two of them having this conversation if she wasn't still, more than a little annoyingly, embarrassed about how she'd behaved earlier.

Not that she expected Bianca to understand, but for whatever godforsaken reason, one she'd never struggled with before, she wanted to be honest.

Maybe it was because Bianca didn't seem to want anything from her that made their tenuous friendship so awkward. There was no angle, at least as far as Maeve could see. Bianca was only being nice and gracious because that was who she was.

Moving over to the bar, Maeve grabbed one of the upturned stools and put it on the ground. After she eased herself into a seated position, she grabbed one of the coasters from behind the bar and flipped it idly through her fingers. So this was what all the customers felt like when they unloaded on their bartenders, like therapy was included because of whatever tip they left.

But, stupidly, she couldn't help it. She didn't want Bianca to be disappointed in her.

With a nervous sound that was so unlike her, she ran her fingers through her wavy locks and took a deep breath. Then she ran her fingers along the six piercings on her left ear in a way that comforted her, gearing herself up to finally speak. One more quick inhale before, "Well, I want to apologize anyway. You were just doing something nice for your boss. I shouldn't have been an asshole about that, especially during work."

She watched Bianca's brows furrow together the slightest bit and wondered what she was thinking. Not what she said, but what she was actually thinking. About Maeve's hot-and-cold act. About how she was a sullen, frustrated mess most of the time. How did she see Maeve, when all Maeve did implied she didn't want to be here?

Slowly, Bianca's lips eased into a soft smile. "I think you're going through a lot. Picking up your life to come back to Kingsford. Losing your mom. Becoming a full-time bartender. Every one of those things would be difficult on its own, and you went right for the hat trick."

"Is that a soccer thing?" Maeve asked, purposefully latching onto exactly the wrong part of Bianca's words.

"No, it's a hockey thing, but something tells me you already know that." Bianca's voice was sincere but strong with her lightly teasing words. Like she had life figured out in a way Maeve felt like she never would, even if she lived to be one hundred.

Maeve smirked instead of having an honest conversation. It was truly a skill. "You can't prove that."

Bianca finished loading the last of the dirty glassware and shut the dishwasher door before turning it on. "Well, if you ever want to talk about any of the aforementioned things, I'm here.

And if you don't, I'm also available to roll our eyes about cheap customers."

"Why?" Maeve hadn't been able to figure out Bianca's angle, and though she didn't consider herself especially suspicious, she figured she may as well ask.

"Because anyone that leaves less than a fifteen percent tip is kind of an asshole?"

Secretly, Maeve kinda liked that they were fucking with one another. It made hard conversations easier, and it was a surprising thing to learn about Bianca, that she had a little more sarcasm than expected.

Even if Maeve only had another month here, she was tired. And though all she wanted to do was curl up and sleep until January when she left, she couldn't.

Every day, she had to get up and see her father, who wasn't making much progress. And she had to come to the bar and deal with idiots, which was more annoying because she couldn't tell them off. And lastly, something she had no intention of admitting out loud, she needed a friend. A very attractive friend was maybe pushing it a little close to the line, but still, people weren't knocking down her door to deal with Misanthropic Maeve (trademark pending).

"You know what I mean. Why do you want to deal with me?" God, could she sound any more pathetic? Being back in Kingsford was really changing her, and not for the better.

"Deal with you?" Bianca asked, genuine confusion in her tone. "I just don't like to see people having a hard time. And I've always felt like things are a little less bleak when we don't feel so alone."

"Wow, I sure must have been making a good impression the last few months."

"I think you're self-aware enough to know that you haven't

been exactly open." Bianca said before adding quickly, "But that's your business. I'm just here if you ever want a friend."

"Does the offer have an expiration?" Maeve asked, trying to push any flirtation from her voice. Which wasn't the easiest thing in the world when a woman like Bianca was searching her face so earnestly.

Bianca ran her tongue along her teeth like she was seriously considering her answer. She put her hands down on the bar and leaned forward, her stare anchoring Maeve in place. Finally, she burst out laughing and grabbed the coaster from Maeve's hand. Pulling a pen from her pocket, she scribbled her number down on the thin cardboard and handed it back. "Honestly, no. Shoot me a text if you ever wanna hang out, and if not, I'll still see you on Fridays."

She didn't know if Bianca realized the sheer amount of game she was projecting right then, but it was causing all kinds of feelings to skitter through Maeve's body.

But maybe Bianca really was just this upfront. And honest. And sincere.

So... if Bianca Rossi wanted to be Maeve's friend, and put no expectations on that offer, who was she to say no?

Chapter Four

On Monday morning, Bianca's phone chimed. Maeve hadn't responded with her own number in return on Friday, so she assumed their weekly workplace proximity associates relationship would continue indefinitely.

She was pleasantly surprised to know that wasn't the case.

518-555-2277 – 8:50 a.m.
Two separate gentlemen callers asked about you on Saturday. I didn't have the heart to tell them you've never worked a Saturday. Is this a common occurrence for you?

Bianca smiled and, after a quick glance around to make sure no one at the vet's office needed her attention, fired off a response.

Bianca Rossi – 8:51 a.m.

Not true. I've worked two Saturdays since I started bartending there.

While she waited for Maeve to respond, she updated her contact details. It made things feel more real somehow.

And she wasn't going to pick apart that the first thing Maeve ever texted her was about the suitors clamoring at her door. There was always a guy with a smooth line, sliding his number across the bartop for her to "give him a call if she wanted to have a good time."

She'd had plenty of good times in her life. That wasn't what she was after anymore.

Smiling instinctively as Maeve's name appeared on-screen, she opened the message quickly.

Maeve Murphy – 8:53 a.m.
That's a flimsy point, but it seems like there's something in the water.

And then Maeve added a couple of little fish emojis for good measure.

It was, quite possibly, the lightest Maeve had ever been with her. Gone was the quiet frustration that usually oozed from the blonde like she was a leaky sieve.

Bianca Rossi – 8:53 a.m.
It's cuffing season.

. . .

Cuffing Season

Bianca responded only seconds after Maeve's text came through. Not that she'd mention unwanted numbers slid her way was an annoyingly common occurrence for her regardless of the time of year.

At least this way she could redirect the conversation.

She had to wait minutes, torturous minutes, for a response, wondering if she'd succeeded.

Maeve Murphy – 8:59 a.m.
WTF is cuffing season?

Bianca laughed and did another quick scan of the waiting room. Their two opening appointments had been taken back twenty minutes ago, and besides the other two customers and their pets waiting to be called back, it was blissfully quiet.

Bianca scrunched her face, her fingers flying across the phone screen. She wrote and then deleted her first few attempts, finally settling on:

Bianca Rossi – 9:00 a.m.
It's like... when it's cold out and people want to be in short relationships to pass the winter months.

Whatever had briefly distracted Maeve before seemed to be gone, and Bianca saw the typing bubbles pop up immediately as a response came through.

Maeve Murphy – 9:01 a.m.

You're fucking with me…

She could picture Maeve saying those words out loud. Besides the initial shock of Maeve's willingness to actually communicate with her, even if it was just over text, this was exactly the response Bianca would expect Maeve to have.

Bianca Rossi – 9:02 a.m.
I promise I'm not. You can look it up yourself.

Maeve Murphy – 9:03 a.m.
How do you know about this? Does everyone know about this?

She imagined Maeve, her lips pursed as she squinted at her screen, trying to figure out if this was some elaborate joke. Maybe she was still in bed, sitting against her pillows, knees pulled up to her elbows as she browsed the internet to confirm that yes, Bianca was telling the truth.

It was one thing Bianca prided herself on. Sometimes she was maybe a little evasive when the situation called for it, but always in service of not hurting someone. Whenever possible, she tried to be honest.

Like, she'd never tell a patient's owner something that would hurt them to know, but she would focus on relaying all the positive attributes of their pet's health and making the conversation as comforting as she could.

Even if she knew that it was a horrible situation, like in cases where an illness or injury was unexpected. Someone could ask her directly in those cases, and she'd still talk around it.

Other than that, she was always honest, and on top of that, she tried to always be positive. It made her feel better about the life she was leading, and there was almost always something good to say, even if that meant leaving the bad things unsaid.

So she'd never tell someone like Maeve that she'd been a little bitchy her first months in town because there was so much going on in Maeve's life and it wouldn't have been helpful. And more than that, there was no right way to respond to grief.

Instead, Bianca had finally, when the chance had presented itself, offered a tenuous olive branch of friendship.

She was more than a little bit surprised that Maeve had finally taken it. Did that mean she was staying in town? Or just that she was so burnt-out with loneliness that she was finally willing to accept someone as her friend?

Maybe one day they'd get to the point that Bianca could ask, but she wasn't going to hold her breath.

And yeah, so maybe Maeve was more than a little attractive, and she'd be the perfect type of person to spend a cuffing season with. But that wasn't what Bianca wanted. And it wasn't what Maeve needed.

She'd thought about seeing Maeve with that woman behind the bar more than a few times over the last few weeks. Remembering what Maeve had looked like, leaned forward with the woman pressed against the brick.

Bianca's stomach still did this annoying little swoop when she thought about how Maeve had pulled her hands out from under the woman's sweater, eyes lidded and then brightening when she realized who'd interrupted them.

Maeve Murphy – 9:07 a.m.

There are *literal* articles about this. God, millennials have a word for everything.

Maeve's message pulled Bianca back to the present, back to her very new friend whom she'd been having very un-friend-like thoughts about.

A message quickly followed after.

Maeve Murphy – 9:08 a.m.
Wait... Are you trying to friendship cuff me? Is that a thing?

I'm... Bianca stopped herself from finishing the thought with an instinctive response because honestly, given the very recent indecent thoughts she'd had, they wouldn't be helpful to add to an already tenuous friendship.

Finally, after retyping over more tries than her self-imposed commitment to honesty should have dictated, she felt like she'd struck a good balance.

Bianca Rossi – 9:11 a.m.
I'm trying to make your time in Kingsford a little less boring.

Maeve Murphy – 9:12 a.m.
Whew. Thank god. This lone wolf can't be tamed. Awoooooo.

. . .

And of course she included a GIF of a tiny wolf howling for good measure.

Until a few weeks ago, Bianca hadn't realized Maeve could be... sweet. And that was even more unsettling.

Never so happy for a customer to come in, she heard the bell chime.

Bianca Rossi – 9:13 a.m.
Have to wrangle a new patient. I'll see you Friday!

She put her phone facedown on her desk and looked up at the person approaching. "Hey there. You have an appointment?"

"Sure do," said the guy who looked about thirty, dressed in a pair of dark jeans and a button-down. Honestly, he was more put together than a lot of the locals she usually saw around town. He had a black lab on a leash, though the dog was already sitting patiently at his side. "I'm Jack Rollins, and my dog, Dennis, has an appointment."

Bianca leaned over the desk to look down at Dennis, who was happily waiting for what came next. God, she wished every pet that came in here could behave like that.

"I don't recognize Dennis. This is your first appointment, correct?"

Jack nodded. "Sure is. We just moved to town. I filled out the paperwork online, and my old vet said they already forwarded Dennis's records to you."

Bianca looked back at her screen and confirmed that yes, everything Jack had said was true. "Looks like we have it all, so if you can take a seat, one of our techs will be out in just a few minutes."

"Will do," Jack said before giving her a smile and walking over to one of the empty chairs, Dennis right in step with him.

Thankfully, the rest of the day passed quickly and with no unexpected situations.

When Bianca got home around five, she gave her mom a call to say hello while she made dinner.

While she talked about her day and all the animals that had come in and then listened to her mom's updates on the family, she thought about Maeve.

What did someone who didn't seem to like this town all that much do on a Monday night off?

* * *

Maeve had friends. Of course she did. There was her favorite bodega guy who always let her shop even if she showed up a few minutes after closing. And though her job could be solitary, there were a couple of recurring people that she worked with on projects for the creative ad agency. A few of the people she'd hooked up with had become what she'd qualify as a friend, though Jade had moved to Atlanta last year and Tegan had moved to San Francisco.

The reality was, there was no expectation of permanence in a place like New York City. A million people there for a million different reasons led to a lot of paths that crossed but didn't stay on the same route.

And she was okay with that. In the constant comparison of quantity versus quality, she was all about meeting as many people as possible. On top of that, it wasn't like with her hours she ever had standing dates or activities with people. It wasn't like she was on call, but she had to be willing to schedule jobs at the client's preferred time, regardless of whether she'd rather be curled up on the sofa with a good book and a bottle of beer.

So why, then, had she made that stupid comment about Bianca trying to friendship cuff her?

Because she was an idiot who probably and truly didn't have many actual friends. So she didn't know how to act around them. Case in point, the message she'd sent yesterday that still caused heat to roll through her body every time she thought about it.

They hadn't texted since, and Maeve wondered if she'd already fucked up something she hadn't even decided she'd wanted until she was right smack dab in the middle of the conversation.

Because she hadn't been planning on texting Bianca. No, when she'd woken up Monday morning, her big plans had been to go to the gym and try to avoid seeing her dad before he went to the bar.

And she'd accomplished both of those tasks.

Then, she'd driven home in the car that used to be her mom's, back to an empty house. The heaviness had settled over her like a fog, and she wanted to escape it.

Simple as that.

Maybe she couldn't call someone up in Kingsford for a nine a.m. booty call, but there was one person who'd expressed an interest in what was going on in Maeve's life.

Bianca.

She wouldn't have broken her self-imposed commitment to keep her at arm's length if she'd had another option. At least, that's what she needed to tell herself. And really, all she was doing was passing along a message.

Because two different guys had honestly asked if Bianca was working on Saturday. And reminding Maeve of that made it easier to separate the Bianca that had watched her outside the bar with curious excitement from the Bianca who was effortlessly sweet and had far more patience than Maeve could begin to comprehend.

So she'd be friends with social butterfly and Kingsford welcoming committee Bianca Rossi.

Problem solved.

Maeve would pass the time a little bit easier, and with Bianca's revolving door of suitors, it would never get weird.

No one had ever commended her for being especially detail-oriented, but she felt like, for how their friendship had started, and barring the slight hiccup with her idiot question, things could be going worse.

Now, all she had to do was not fuck it up. God, she almost wished she had to work tonight to take her mind off of how difficult acting like a normal person was.

***

"Bianca, where the hell have you been, loca?"

Bianca was already grinning when she looked up. Her best friend, Jonny, was leaning out of his car window, beckoning her over.

They'd met when Bianca had been relatively new to town, right after she'd gotten her job at the vet's office. He'd brought in his cat, Edward, for a routine exam, and the cat's namesake had come up quickly, mostly because Jonny had felt the need to explain it to her.

Because, knowing Jonny now, it made perfect sense that he had named his pet after a *Twilight* character. It's also why he insisted on giving her the same greeting every time he saw her. It didn't matter if it was like now, in the parking lot of a grocery store, or when it was sometimes inappropriate, like at her places of business.

"How's the life of a fabulous accountant?" Bianca asked, walking toward the driver's side window.

"Well, no one's watching the newest season of *Real Housewives*, but I'm so damn good at my job they still pretend to listen when I talk about it."

"None of them?" Bianca asked in mock horror.

He gestured into the car. "Sit your ass inside and we can chat for a few minutes. I was just driving by and couldn't miss the chance to say hi to my future baby mama."

Bianca rolled her eyes but walked around to the side of the car and got in. Maybe one day, via a lab if neither of them found a person to settle down with.

"Why is it so cold?" she asked, putting her hands against the fans on the dashboard, which were pumping heat at full blast. She'd only been outside for the short walk from the store to the car, then for thirty seconds more while she loaded her groceries in the trunk of her SUV.

"Just one of those winters, I guess. The river's already freezing in some spots and it's barely December. Batten down the hatches and load up on hot cocoa, it's gonna be a cold one," he finished, his voice a spot-on impersonation of an on-air meteorologist

She continued rubbing her numb fingers together in front of the heater while Jonny pulled into the empty spot next to hers. "Global warming is a misnomer," she said. "Some places are getting hotter and some are getting colder, which is why climate change is a more accurate term for modern use."

Jonny looked at her like she'd sprouted another head. "B, are you fucking kidding me? Please do not tell me these are the kind of conversation topics you bring up on dates. No wonder you're still single." He gave her a once-over before adding, "Which is a travesty because damn, girl, you are F-I-N-E. Did you do something new with your hair?"

She raised her finger. They'd had this conversation more than once. "First of all, I wouldn't want to be with anyone who wouldn't talk to me about climate change."

"And what's second? I know there's a second."

Bianca scrunched her nose at him. Sometimes, she felt like he was actively trying to drive her insane. "Obviously there's a second. Why would I have said first if there wasn't a second?"

He bumped their shoulders together. "Girl, lighten up. What's got your panties in a twist?"

"Nothing," she said quickly, her attention distracted as someone walked past the front of the car.

Because of course.

Jonny followed Bianca's stare. "So she eats—like actual real food. Or at least that's what she wants us to believe. I figured she only came out at night to feed on the blood of the weak."

This was Bianca's fault, she realized. That she'd mentioned once or twice over the past few months that Maeve was a difficult person to know.

"That's a shitty thing to say, Jonny." She knew it wouldn't stop him. It never did.

"Well, no one gives my girl the brushoff and gets away without a tongue lashing."

"That you would never dare say to her face."

He gave her a side-eye. "I don't think I'm the one she'd want a tongue lashing from, if you get my drift."

"Subtle, Jonny," she said, even as she felt her cheeks heat up.

He smirked and watched as Maeve headed into the store before turning his attention back to Bianca. "I have excellent gaydar. And that woman is G-A-Y. Just because she's immune to your charms, I'm sorry to tell you, doesn't make it any less true."

Bianca shook her head. She didn't want to go down this

path with him. She loved Jonny, but he was like a dog with a bone. "Actually, we're, like... sort of becoming friends maybe?"

His eyebrows lifted so high they almost disappeared under his perfectly coiffed Caesar bangs. "Shut the fuck up. Why did you not lead with that?"

"It's new. Honestly, it may not even stick. She's a little... all over the place when it comes to her willingness to engage." She debated telling Jonny this next part, but there was no point in keeping secrets from him. "I gave her my number on Friday, as a friend," she emphasized, "and she texted me this morning."

If Jonny had popcorn right then, he'd have been shoveling it into his face by the fistful. "What about?"

"To tell me that two guys had asked about me on Saturday night."

"So she's testing the waters," he said immediately.

She shook her head. "No. That's not what she's doing. And anyway, I told her it's cuffing season and this is a terrible time to respond to potential love interests."

Jonny's exuberant laugh echoed off the interior of the car. "Oh god. This is too good. So she tries to see if you're interested in men, and you volley it back with a seasons-based blanket dating refusal."

"That's not..." Bianca took a second to compose herself. Jonny really had a way with words, and the only way she was getting out of this was slowly and steadily. "I think you're jumping to a lot of conclusions."

"Jumpin' dem bones is more like it."

"Jonny," she said sharply. The smirk dropped from his face instantly. "Maeve's mom died less than a year ago, and her entire life was upended when she came back here to help her dad. I'm not trying to work some kind of game on her, and I don't think that's the case for her either. Say what you want to me, but never ever bring this up if you talk to her." She gave him a withering look. "Got it?"

He looked properly chastised. "Got it. You're a good person, B. I sometimes forget that."

"And you are too." She shot him a smile. "You just let your mouth run away instead of your mind."

"Wanna do dinner this week?" She could tell he was trying to get back in her good graces, and she loved him for it. What he lacked in his initial behavior, he more than made up for with a willingness to do better next time.

"Sure."

"Great. Remember that you already committed and how much you love me and that I only have your best interests at heart."

"What?"

* * *

"Maeve!"

It was her name, undoubtedly, but she didn't know who the man was yelling at her from a silver Audi SUV in the grocery store parking lot at six p.m.

But if he wanted to kidnap her, maybe it wouldn't be the worst thing in the world to have a change of scenery.

She clutched the paper bag in her hands a little tighter as she reached the front of the car and looked through the windshield.

A window opened on the passenger's side. "Hey, Maeve. Sorry if Jonny scared the shit out of you."

Right, Bianca's friend Jonny. She'd seen them together at Murph's a few times when Bianca wasn't working. They'd have dinner, and Jonny would order some garishly sweet drink that pained her to make. Why drink if you couldn't even taste the alcohol?

She walked around to Bianca's side, eye level with her in the SUV. "Hey?"

"So, Maeve," Jonny said, launching into whatever he was about to say with gusto. "I was going to watch a movie that Bianca's been dying to see with her tomorrow night, but I'm unexpectedly unavailable. You interested in filling in?"

Maeve felt more than a little trapped right now—or, at the very least, she felt like she was being led into a trap. To what end, she wasn't sure.

She looked through the car at Jonny, who seemed far too pleased with himself. And when she shifted her stare to Bianca, rigid in her seat, it was difficult to parse out the look clouding her green eyes.

Finally, after an uncomfortable few seconds passed among the three of them, Bianca spoke up, her face flushed in a way that Maeve didn't want to find as cute as she did. "Obviously, you're more than welcome to watch a movie with me tomorrow night, but you shouldn't feel obligated in any way. Jonny is just mother-henning me for no good reason. He means well, but please ignore him at your discretion."

Maeve lifted a brow and gave Jonny a quick glance before looking at Bianca again. She didn't know what had overtaken her body, but the words that came out weren't the ones she'd expected to say. "Getting out of the house sounds like a good idea. Otherwise, it's just a night of listening to my dad watch sports with the TV on too loudly."

Jonny honest to god clapped his hands together. "Well, that's settled then. Anyway, Maeve, it's nice to meet you officially."

"Likewise, Jonny," she said flatly.

That earned an appreciative laugh from Bianca, who punched him in the arm. "She's got your number, Jonny."

"It's about time someone in this damn town can go toe to toe with me," he responded, undeterred.

"Okay... well..." Maeve bounced back and forth, trying not to focus on the pressing sensation of all the heat leaving her body.

"I'll text you the address?" Bianca said softly, arresting Maeve's attention.

She nodded. "Sure."

With a quick wave, Maeve headed back to her car and jumped in the driver's side. The last three minutes felt like some sort of hallucination in which she'd accepted an invitation to go to Bianca's house like their moms had planned a playdate for them.

A slightly uncomfortable feeling settled in her stomach, like she'd eaten an ill-advised taquito from the gas station at the edge of town.

Guess she'd see what all this "friends" business was about sooner than later.

Chapter Five

"Chili's on the stove for dinner."

Maeve looked up to see her dad, dressed in a rumpled flannel, leaning against the doorframe of the kitchen.

"Thanks, but I'm going out tonight." She didn't clarify further, and he didn't ask. She'd only come out of her room to grab a glass of water, still about thirty minutes until she was supposed to leave to go to Bianca's house.

"All right then. I'm gonna go to Duke's and watch the game." He never specified which game, not that it mattered to Maeve.

"Sure thing. See you later," she said with a weak wave.

And that was how their conversations mostly went. They didn't talk about her mom. They didn't talk about anything really, unless it was about the bar. At this point, she thought, they should just leave sticky notes on the fridge instead of going through these short yet painful interactions.

Seconds later, she heard the front door open and close, followed by the sound of his old truck sputtering to life.

The day had gone by quickly, but that made sense, since

she'd done everything possible to avoid thinking about her *friend's hangout* later that night.

Early that morning, even beating the over-sixty crowd to the gym, she'd run until she knew she'd be sore the next day. After a shower that she'd intended to be quick but had morphed into using all the hot water because the warmth had just felt so damn nice, she'd put on loungewear and gotten down to the business of planning her escape from Kingsford.

Her portfolio was updated, including some shots she'd taken over the summer when it hadn't physically pained her to be outside. A few agencies were looking for seasonal help, so even though she wasn't going to apply, she was starting to get a read on what was out there. She'd sent a quick email to her contact at the creative agency, inquiring about their work in the new year.

And then, because it was easy, she'd watched a few mind-numbing hours of television on her laptop. She liked things dark and twisty, stuff that encompassed the breadth of human emotion.

As her day would have normally come to a close, retreating back in her room with a bowl of her dad's impressively good chili, not that she'd admit that to him, she found herself, instead, shrugging off her leggings and surveying her closet.

Maeve didn't tend to worry all that much about what people thought of her. So she was finding herself more than a little bit irritated as she flipped through the shirts in her closet and tried to find one that worked.

Whenever she had a shift, she wore black jeans and a black shirt. And she could count on one hand the number of times she'd had to get dressed to go anywhere other than work or the gym since coming back to Kingsford.

Bianca probably wouldn't be impressed with her leather bomber jacket, which she loved to wear out in New York City on cold winter nights. And really, there was no point in putting on makeup since this was just a casual night at home.

Truly, what bothered her most was that in New York City, she didn't have nights like this. She didn't go to people's apartments—no one that she knew had a house—and just *hung out*.

Why pay an exorbitant amount of money to live in a city if you weren't going to enjoy it?

And it annoyed her that she felt so out of sorts, that she couldn't find her bearings on what to expect.

Maybe because she didn't really know what she wanted? The idea of being alone with Bianca, no buffer between the two of them, made her a little nervous if she was being honest with herself.

She didn't talk. She got out and did things. And tonight, there was nothing to do.

God, she was making herself feel crazy.

"This is stupid," she muttered into the empty room.

Grabbing a shirt and pants from her closet, she threw them on the bed and forced herself to get ready instead of agonizing over it for another second.

* * *

Bianca hadn't known what Maeve being in her house would be like. Which was why, more than once but hopefully less than a dozen times, she'd snuck glances at Maeve, who sat on the sofa and took small sips of the beer she'd accepted upon arrival.

Maeve was dressed casually in a way that absolutely worked for her. She wore dark skinny jeans with a white V-neck T-shirt that had a heavy flannel layered on top. Bianca wondered if the flannel was as soft as it looked, and she resisted running her fingers along the gently frayed cuffs that were rolled up around Maeve's forearms.

"So, what'd you do today? Day off, right?" Bianca clarified unnecessarily, pulling her focus from the clean line of muscle displayed when Maeve flexed her fingers around the beer bottle she held.

Maeve rolled the edges of the bottle before picking gingerly at the edge of the label. When she turned her attention away from her fingers, her blue eyes were light but guarded. She was wearing less makeup than she did for shifts at the bar, but Bianca could see the faint traces of mascara on Maeve's impossibly long eyelashes and smudgy hints of eyeliner at the corners of her eyes.

"Gym in the morning. Then I caught up on some stuff to prepare for heading back to New York City."

Right. Because Maeve was leaving. And Bianca knew that. She'd been told that, more than once, by Maeve herself. Their friendship was so new and tentative that she didn't know why hearing it again shot an empty feeling to the pit of her stomach.

She took a small sip of her own beer. "After the new year, right?"

"That's the plan," Maeve said with a sigh. "I gave up my room in the apartment I was subletting from before coming back." Maeve's brows drew together in concentration. "Actually, that's not true. I kept it for two months and paid rent before realizing that my dad needed the extra help around here. Then I gave it up."

"Oh," Bianca said, acknowledging Maeve's words but hoping that she'd say more, not wanting to veer the conversation off in another direction.

She was surprised when her wish was answered. "So the logistics of getting back to the city are a little complicated. I don't want to get another room until I can secure some new work, but I don't want to get work if I'd have to commute back into the city from here."

"Got it. Do you have any friends you could stay with while you get back in the swing of things?" She chastised herself immediately. Obviously Maeve would have already thought of that.

"The apartment I was living in had four bedrooms, so it's possible one will open up again soon. I wasn't especially tight with anyone, but they were all functional adults with jobs, so that's pretty much the pinnacle of cohabitation as far as I'm concerned."

"I definitely remember those days," Bianca said sincerely.

Maeve shot her a curious look. "Living with roommates?" She glanced around the small but well-decorated house that Bianca lived in, just a few blocks from Maeve's own. Which she knew because she'd stopped by with her dad once or twice. "I didn't realize Kingsford was in such a housing crisis."

Bianca rolled her eyes playfully. "I lived in New York City. I actually grew up in Brooklyn, and then I went to college in the city. But after both my parents retired, they moved to Kingsford the year before I graduated. I was doing some work in the city, so I decided to stay. I made it for about a year after I finished up school before I decided I wanted to move up here and join them."

It was kind of adorable how confused Maeve looked when she asked, genuinely, "So you were born in New York City and lived there, with a built-in social network and everything..." She could see Maeve trying to find the right words. "And you decided to come here? To hang out with your retired parents?"

Bianca didn't take any offense to her words. Honestly, Jonny had asked her exactly the same thing. "I love my family... but also, the city really wasn't for me." Her stare tracked back to Maeve's fingers, back to toying with the piece of beer bottle label she'd freed.

"That's just... wild to me," Maeve admitted. "What work did you do in the city?"

She knew her cheeks had grown redder. This wasn't a conversation she ever tried to bring up with people, mostly because it made them look at her differently. "I did a little modelling. Nothing serious, but enough to pay my bills. And, well, at first, it seemed stupid to give up something fairly lucrative..."

It settled something in her that Maeve didn't look at her like she'd suddenly decided Bianca was dumb or vain because of what she'd found out. "But?"

"Well, I mean... it kind of has an expiration date, right? And people have a lot of assumptions about it, but it's not easy. Boring sometimes, yes. But it's surprisingly physically demanding. On top of that, people make inferences..."

Maeve's lips quirked into a smile, more playful than anything. Bianca resisted thinking about how much she liked seeing it. "Oh yeah?"

Bianca rolled her eyes. "See? So the reality is that I'd rather live with my family in a small town and work a normal job than be constantly judged for my looks and have people think I'm an airhead."

When she'd left the city, her model friends had thought she was insane. Who left when you were still on the upward swing? She'd only been twenty-three, and bigger brands had been starting to notice her. But there was also a part of her friends that had seemed relieved, like she was nothing more than another competitor out of the running for a finite number of jobs. She'd stayed in touch with a few of them, but with their differences in lifestyles these days, the relationships had drifted away naturally.

The saddest part was that Bianca couldn't say she missed

them all that much. Once the veneer of work and social events had been stripped away, they didn't have a lot else in common.

And she absolutely didn't miss the way people looked at her once they found out about her job.

Sure, Maeve was... regarding her, for lack of a better word, but it was like she was trying to understand Bianca more than anything else. Like she genuinely cared what she had to say. And, most importantly, like Bianca wasn't a conquest to be achieved.

"I've done some portraits for clients. You have a great bone structure, so the modelling makes sense." Maeve's words were more matter-of-fact than anything, but that didn't stop the little thrill Bianca felt as her eyes tracked across her features.

Ah, so that was it. The regard was professional, which was probably for the best.

"So... how is Kingsford stacking up to your expectations then?" There was that half smile again when Maeve asked, the one that Bianca was already growing a little addicted to, given the flutter it caused in her abdomen.

Bianca smiled. "Pretty good. My two older brothers, Andrea and Franco, still live in the city, but they come up at least once a month for dinner on Sundays. And I love my job at the vet's office. I work with great people who are the perfect balance between mindless chatter and checking in with me." She sighed happily before adding the next part. "And I'm so proud of my dad. I know he was a little lost when he retired from firefighting, and I'm so happy he has the chance to share his love of cooking with people."

Maeve is a good listener Bianca thought. They'd turned their bodies toward one another, and Maeve had moved her sock-clad foot onto the sofa, resting her elbow on her knee, all of her focus on what Bianca was saying.

"But I'm talking a lot," Bianca said, a little embarrassed so that she pushed the words out quickly.

"It's fine," Maeve said, clearing her throat. She paused for a moment, her eyes dimming slightly. "It's nice to hear someone else's words instead of the thoughts pinging around endlessly in my own head."

"Well, consider me here to fill the void then."

Maeve lifted her eyebrow to indicate the accidental implication wasn't lost on her, but she didn't mention it. "I do have a question, though…"

A smile spread across Bianca's face in spite of the little zings of embarrassment that kept popping up when she thought about what she'd just said. Because she liked when Maeve asked her questions, blue eyes trained intently on her. "And what's that?"

An exasperated little noise pushed itself free from Maeve's throat when she said, "Does everyone *really* know about cuffing season?"

* * *

When Maeve glanced down at her phone resting on the coffee table, a notification popped up. She ignored it, but was surprised to see that she'd already been at Bianca's for an hour.

Then again, a lot about tonight had been a surprise. Bianca, showing up at the door in a pair of comfy leggings and a crewneck sweatshirt that hung off her shoulder. It accentuated her exposed collarbone, her hair pulled up in a messy bun atop her head instead of the standard high ponytail she wore to bartend.

She looked… relaxed. And, a little unfairly, just as gorgeous as when she was done up for her Friday night shifts in her painted-on black jeans and tight black shirts.

Maeve felt like if a person saw Bianca dressed to the nines, they'd immediately think, *Yeah, that's how she should look.* Natural beauty elevated to an almost ethereal level with a few brushes of makeup and a flattering outfit.

And maybe Maeve had thought that an hour ago too.

But now, it was hard to imagine Bianca any other way than with her legs on the sofa, pulled toward her, with her head resting gently on her knees. Little wisps of her soft hair had escaped her bun and floated delicately around her face.

Tightening her hand around her beer bottle, Maeve resisted smoothing them back against Bianca's temple.

A few minutes ago, Bianca had settled into the sofa again after running to the kitchen for another round of beers and to make a bowl of popcorn.

"I believe you promised to explain cuffing season to me," Maeve said as she placed her beer bottle down on a coaster.

Bianca let out a light, low laugh. "You can blame Jonny for telling me what it was."

"He's a character," Maeve settled on, keeping her voice neutral. She didn't especially like men yelling at her from cars, regardless of their intentions. But Bianca seemed to have a good sense of people, so she was trying to reserve judgment.

"But in this case... he's spot-on, right? I mean, think about it," Bianca continued, her eyes sparkling excitedly. "It makes perfect sense. It gets dark so early. And people don't want to go out in the freezing cold. It's nice to just have someone to spend some time with in comfy, oversized clothes and escape from the winter for a little while."

Maeve was already starting to like how whenever Bianca felt like she'd overshared, a faint blush spread across her cheeks.

"So, do you have a moratorium on dating during the winter then? Or is that perfect for what you're looking for?" Regardless of the season, she'd never seen Bianca do anything with the phone numbers she was given other than throwing them discreetly in the trash.

And maybe she was a little unhelpfully curious about what Bianca's deal was, romantically speaking.

Bianca pulled her lower lip between her teeth and chewed on it for a second before letting it go. "I'm over the casual hookup stage of my life." What a shame for Maeve.

"Which means?"

"That I'm looking for something serious, but I'm not trying to force it. I'd be lying though if I said it wasn't important to me."

Maeve would have been more pleased that she'd been spot-on with her assessment of Bianca as a hopeless romantic if she wasn't so disappointed by it.

"So... you moved from one of the most populated cities in the United States to Kingsford when your goal is to meet someone?"

"When you say it like that..."

"How would you say it?"

"It just... it felt like in the city, no one wanted to settle down. Everyone was chasing something, someone. There were too many options."

It was an explanation Maeve understood perfectly, though usually she benefited from it. Still, it didn't seem like the worst hardship in the world to curl up with someone like Bianca every night. No, not at all.

She shook the thought away as quickly as it had flitted through her mind. "So, what's the movie you're just dying to watch?"

Cheeks splashed with an unmistakable tinge of heat, Bianca tapped her fingers against her knees. "Oh god. Honestly, we don't have to watch it. I mostly just made popcorn because I was hungry."

Maeve inched a little closer, a smile playing on her lips. "Let me guess. A cheesy holiday romance movie?"

"It's not as bad as it sounds. Do I secretly enjoy them? Yes. But when Jonny comes over, we watch them and laugh and give commentary on how improbably it all falls together."

"Like how? I've never watched one." And probably wouldn't have been caught dead watching one with anyone except the woman next to her. Who, for reasons still a little unclear to Maeve, had already done a very good job of breaking through some of Maeve's defenses.

Bianca's face lit up. "Seriously? Not even in a 'so bad it's good but still bad' kind of way?"

"Maybe with my mom when I was younger?" she said, a twinge of sadness evident in her voice. She hadn't even remembered the memory until the words had come out.

"Hey..." She felt Bianca's warm hand wrap around her own. "This was just supposed to be a fun way to escape for a while. We can absolutely watch something else if it doesn't feel right."

Maeve shook her head emphatically. "It's honestly not a big deal."

It was hard to look anywhere else but at the intensity in Bianca's green eyes. She held Maeve's stare for a few beats before she seemed to accept the truth in Maeve's words. Or, that even if she didn't think they were true, she wasn't going to push it. "Okay. But, it's still very important that we make fun of it. It's, like... central to the process."

"There's a process?" Maeve asked, her brow arching upward.

"Sure is." Bianca's voice oozed confidence as she turned away from Maeve and propped her feet up. She stretched her body forward and plucked the remote off the coffee table and turned on the TV. "But don't worry," she said, shooting Maeve a disarming grin. "I will be happy to guide you."

There was no world in which Maeve thought this was how any woman would be *guiding* her, but she was finding that, already, when it was Bianca suggesting it, she was much more inclined to agree.

Maeve knew a slippery slope when she saw it, but if she kept the important things in the forefront of her mind, it would all be fine. Bianca was straight. And Bianca was looking for something serious. And Maeve was leaving in less than a month.

So maybe... a good friendship cuffing season, if that was even a thing, was exactly what Maeve needed to get through the rest of her time in Kingsford in one piece.

Chapter Six

On Friday night, Bianca showed up thirty minutes early for her shift at Murph's, just to make sure everything was ready for the engagement party.

And yeah, maybe it was also a little bit to steal some extra time with Maeve. Who'd, after hanging out with her on Tuesday night, had been exactly what Bianca had expected her to be like, but also not.

Because Maeve had ended up with fewer sarcastic remarks and more commentary on how the holiday movie they'd watched had been filmed. And once she'd gotten into the movie, it had been like nothing else existed. Bianca was almost sure that Maeve hadn't heard the majority of the comments she'd made, her attention focused completely on the TV.

And that had given Bianca a little bit of time to watch Maeve, unguarded while she sat in Bianca's living room like it was a completely natural thing for her to be doing.

She looked at home there, at least as far as Bianca thought. Once they'd gotten over the initial getting-to-know-you conversation, things had flowed between them, more so than with anyone else she'd met recently.

Maeve could end up being a good friend for the rest of the time she was here, and that had to be good enough.

After Bianca threw her coat in a closet at the end of the hallway, she saw her dad pop up from the basement where the kitchen was located.

"Hi, baby," he said cheerfully. Sal Rossi, in spite of his six-foot-plus frame, was a complete teddy bear. "I was just coming up to confirm tonight's party with Patty."

Bianca pointed back to where she'd come from. "He was in the office when I walked by."

He gave her a kiss on the head and moved quietly through the bar before disappearing down the hallway.

When she looked up, Bianca caught Maeve's eye. Maeve looked exactly the same as she always did, in the same type of outfit they both wore when they worked. Maeve usually wore her hair down and tousled, falling just below her shoulders. She always looked a little serious, but after finally seeing her smile, Bianca realized that she had a little dimple in her left cheek that sometimes came out.

So when Maeve smiled at her, the dimple appearing prominently, easily, Bianca stupidly hoped that their friendship had something to do with that. And she hoped that the comfort they'd struck up with one another on Tuesday would exist even at work.

Bianca slipped behind the bar and stood next to Maeve, their arms almost brushing but not quite. "I would say happy Friday, but this is kinda the middle of your work week, so it feels a little lame."

Turning toward her, Maeve leaned her forearm on the bar, inching into Bianca's personal space in a way she felt like she should mind but didn't. She could admit to herself that she liked when Maeve was close. "I don't love working on the weekends, but there is something almost comforting about having regularly scheduled days. I always know that I have Monday and Tuesday off."

"A structured schedule... how utterly banal of you," Bianca teased.

Maeve slid the bar towel resting over her shoulder down in a fluid motion before lightly slapping it in Bianca's direction. "Don't let my secrets get out. First the"—she lowered her voice to a register that Bianca felt through her entire body—"happy holiday movie, and now the love of schedules? What will the other New Yorkers think?"

Bianca focused on the moment, rife with light teasing, instead of the heat slinking down her spine. She liked playful Maeve. A lot. "I do remember there being a test every year to keep your New Yorker card, so I hope I don't get asked any tough questions about you."

Maeve's blue eyes were bright, her grin a little mischievous. "I've still got staying up until two a.m. going for me, though not for fun reasons anymore."

Holding her hand up to her mouth, Bianca let out a quiet gasp. "Maeve Murphy, did you just make a sex joke?"

With a shrug, Maeve stood up straighter again. "I've got to find some way to pass the time here."

Absorbing Maeve's words, Bianca forced herself to remember who she was talking to. "Well, maybe your friend from the other week will return, and you'll get a shot at redemption."

A strange look flitted across Maeve's face, and Bianca felt like she'd walked out on a frozen pond, misjudging it and feeling the echoing crack of ice beneath her.

"Yeah, maybe," Maeve responded after a few beats. She shifted her focus over to the large booth where the engagement party would be taking place. When she tracked her stare back at Bianca, the look was gone. "Let's just focus on getting through the party tonight, and maybe then I can prioritize other... needs."

Well, that didn't help Bianca's imagination.

* * *

The dinner portion of the Kent-McKinley engagement party was almost done, and Maeve was keeping a close eye on the dishes to be ready to clear them.

She watched for another few minutes before gesturing for Liam, the busser who worked on weekend nights, to clear the table.

Maeve could still remember the first time she'd seen Quinn and Sawyer at the bar. It was only about a month after her mom had passed away, so it was strange that she remembered anything. But for whatever reason, they'd stuck out to her.

Quinn had looked sophisticated, sitting ramrod straight on the barstool and clocking every inch of the space. Except when Sawyer hadn't been paying attention, and then Quinn had been looking at her.

Maeve had recognized that look for what it was: longing.

And as they'd had dinner, they'd shifted progressively closer to one another, and Maeve had caught their stares, more than once when she'd come to check on them, lingering on one another's lips.

Sawyer, whom she'd seen before, albeit alone at the restaurant, had seemed to want to look anywhere except at Quinn. Maeve must have watched her read the drinks and specials menu on the chalkboard above the bar at least a dozen times that night.

So even if Maeve wasn't at all hokey or sentimental, there

was a part of her that felt like she was a part of their story in some small way.

Once Liam cleared the tiramisu plates, she eased around the edge of the bar and headed toward them. In doing her best as the daughter of the owner, she'd tried to be more chipper than normal, checking in frequently and chatting with the party.

Which was how she found herself at half past eight with her arm leaning against the edge of the booth where Quinn and Sawyer sat together.

"How was dinner?" she asked.

"Really good," Sawyer answered, lifting her napkin from her thighs and placing it on top of the table.

Maeve noticed how Quinn's hand effortlessly found Sawyer's and interlaced their fingers.

Quinn looked at Sawyer for a beat longer before pulling her focus back to Maeve. "It was excellent. I'm really glad you were able to accommodate us. I know this isn't your usual type of event."

Waving her off with a laugh, Maeve scanned the room quickly. It was one of their busiest nights, but not so loud that it was difficult to hear yourself talk. And it was still early enough that people weren't hanging out behind the seats at the bar for standing room.

When she was confident that everything was under control, she focused her attention back on the couple. "We're happy we could support you two. My dad's still here, back in his office, but I'm sure he'll come out to say hello."

"He greeted us when we arrived," Sawyer answered, her bright eyes dimming the slightest bit. "How are you both doing?"

Most people who lived in Kingsford year-round knew what had happened, so she shouldn't have been surprised. But still, a puff of air stuck in her throat before she swallowed it down and smiled again. "I mean, that's not the kind of conversation we need to be having at a happy event like this."

"It would be if the answer was positive," Quinn said quietly, her smile soft.

Maeve didn't need anyone's pity, but she'd walked right into that one. "Fair," she conceded, letting her smile falter for a second. She liked that Quinn didn't pull any punches.

Quinn seemed to realize she didn't want to talk about it and thankfully changed the subject. "Your dad told us you used to live in New York City. Photography, right?"

"Yeah, and I guess I still do, technically?" she questioned, both to herself and to the women in front of her. "I came back to help after everything, but the plan's to go back eventually."

"It's a great place to live," Quinn said with a wry smile before squeezing Sawyer's hand and adding, "but I can't say I mind where I ended up."

Sawyer lifted their interlaced fingers up and kissed Quinn's hand. "She's being dramatic," she said lovingly. "We go to the city probably once a month, if not more."

"Oh?" Maeve asked, surprise evident in her voice.

Quinn nodded. "I have a few new clients in New York City who've purchased homes in the region, so sometimes I meet them there. Mostly, though, I tag along with Sawyer to estate sales."

A look passed between them that had Sawyer blushing, but neither clarified what it meant.

"That's right. You just opened your new store last month. Congratulations." Maeve remembered seeing the signs for the new antique store in a Victorian house near the edge of the promenade. "Great location."

"Thanks," Sawyer beamed. "It was my grandparents' house, the ones who started the original Kent Antiques. These first few months will basically be a soft opening so we can get everything set up come springtime when things pick up. A lot of my business happens online with collectors across the country, but I wanted a brick-and-mortar location too."

"What about the downtown location?" Maeve asked, trying to remember if she'd heard anything about the other location shutting down.

"Oh," Sawyer said with a sheepish grin. She pointed toward the other end of the table where a man who was undoubtedly a relative of Sawyer's sat with a teenage boy next to him. "My brother owned the original Kent Antiques. I bought the naming rights a few months ago, along with his existing inventory. He wanted to get out of the antiques world, and he's using the capital to start an auto repair shop."

"You should stop by one day," Quinn said, her hazel eyes focused on Maeve in a way that made her wonder what exactly the other woman was seeing. "It's not a bad way to spend a winter day."

Maeve nodded, and when she did another quick glance around the room, she noticed that Bianca was looking at her. She managed a small smile and said, "I'll do that," as she pulled her attention back to Sawyer and Quinn.

Sawyer suddenly got a very excited look on her face, and she pulled out a business card and handed it to Maeve. "I know you're super busy, and it probably won't be exciting work, but I'm looking for someone to help me photograph all the pieces I bought. It's one of the winter projects I'm working on."

Quinn rolled her eyes and laughed. "Love what you do, and you'll never work a day in your life... even at your own engagement party."

Maeve hadn't really considered trying to pick up any freelance work here. Being at the bar had monopolized a lot of her time, but she was itching to get behind a camera again. Inconveniently, freezing temperatures hadn't afforded her much of an opportunity the past month.

She tucked the business card in her pocket. "I'll probably have some time over the next few weeks. I'd love to take a look at what you have and see how I can help."

Sawyer was practically beaming. "Awesome."

After thanking them again, Maeve walked back to the bar and busied herself with the new drink orders that were piling up in her absence. Bianca was at the other end, chatting with Quinn's sister, who'd found her way to a barstool and was talking animatedly with her hands.

There were some things, Maeve could admit, that were nice about small towns. She shook her head. It was probably just her lingering excitement from the prospect of her first photography job in months.

* * *

Around ten p.m., Bianca walked the Kent-McKinley party to the front door. Trevor, Kelly's husband, had taken their daughters home hours ago, and all the parents of the brides along with Sawyer's brother and nephew had left not long after that.

Then Sawyer, Quinn, and Kelly had proceeded to throw back at least three more bottles of wine among the three of them.

"Glad you made tonight count, Kelly," Bianca said as her friend bumped into her on the way to the door.

Quinn and Sawyer had their arms around one another, and Bianca had seen them sneak kisses more than a few times as the night had progressed. She was glad they'd enjoyed it while they could because she doubted there'd be anything except a night of snoring ahead for both of them.

Still, she sighed when Sawyer slipped her hand in Quinn's,

and Quinn smiled when Sawyer whispered something in her ear.

Yeah, she wanted that. And even if she didn't have it yet, she was still so goddamn happy when other people found it.

When the three of them were safely in a taxi—because she didn't care if it was only a fifteen-minute walk home—she headed back behind the bar, which was still absolutely packed.

Families were gone now, and it was groups of mostly younger adults who sat around the tables or watched the TVs they'd turned on behind the bar after the dinner rush had left.

Maeve was moving a mile a minute, slinging drinks and chatting with customers between the million other things she did that helped the bar run. Bianca had always been impressed with Maeve, but she was doubly so tonight after Bianca had seen how good she was with Quinn and Sawyer. So good, that she'd noticed Sawyer hand Maeve her business card at one point.

She wondered what that was about, trying not to give it more weight than deserved. Maeve didn't want to stay in Kingsford, and it was unlikely she'd do anything that encouraged just that.

Instead of letting her imagination run wild, which had already gotten her into trouble tonight, she gave Maeve a quick smile as she returned to her side of the bar.

Most of her seats had turned over, so she started taking a new round of orders. When she got halfway down her section, she recognized a familiar face. "Dennis's dad?" she said, putting a coaster down in front of him.

He did a double take and looked around, like he'd found himself in the wrong place. "From the vet's office, right?" he asked, running his fingers through his hair.

"During the daylight hours, and I work here on Fridays. I'm

Bianca," she said while she poured a beer from the tap in front of her.

"Jack. And yes, father of Dennis." He was cute, Bianca could admit. And to his credit, it was after ten and he didn't seem the least bit drunk.

Bianca put the beer down in front of the person next to him. "Nice to see you again, Jack. What can I get you?"

"Anything local on tap." His gaze settled on Bianca while she continued to work, but it wasn't predatory, unlike some of the guys she had to contend with. She didn't know how Maeve did it five nights a week.

"We switched in a new keg about twenty minutes ago. You good with a lager?"

"Sure am." She noticed a slight drawl in his words she hadn't picked up on the last time they'd met.

"Where'd you move from? You're new in town, right?"

Jack nodded and accepted the beer she'd poured. "Atlanta. I just accepted a job with the city as a project manager."

"And how is Dennis dealing with his relocation?"

A sincere smile worked its way across his face. "Honestly, he loves it. I have a yard and way more space than we had in Atlanta. So far, so good, but you'll be my first call if anything's amiss." When Bianca gave him a strange look, he clarified quickly, "Not you, *you*. The vet's office, I mean. Because, you know, that's where you take dogs that aren't well."

Bianca laughed and tried to shake the embarrassment from her face. She was so used to people hitting on her that she'd mistaken his intent. "Right. That is something we could help with."

"Well, thank you." He held up his beer and then pointed over to a table. "I'm here with some people from work, so I guess I should head back. But it was nice seeing you again."

"You too, Jack." She liked that there wasn't much fanfare to him, that instead of monopolizing her time, he grabbed his beer and cleared the spot for the person behind him, who'd already slipped into the empty seat.

Bianca already knew it was going to be one of those nights, one where she was so tired that she'd fall into bed without an ounce of strength left in her. And it was possible that for the rest of the weekend, after basking in the overwhelming love between Quinn and Sawyer, she'd do nothing except relax and watch as many sappy holiday movies as her heart could handle.

Chapter Seven

Maeve had made a horrible decision. Grabbing coffee while she was still sweaty from the gym was a bad play, and she was paying for it by imagining the ecosystem of bacteria that was growing inside of her puffy jacket right now.

But as she waited for her turn in line at the local coffee shop on Sunday morning, she dug in her heels and decided to push through. It wasn't like she cared that her face was red from exertion. Or that she had a scowl on that was keeping anyone with the smallest amount of sense away from her.

Her life was about simple indulgences these days, and at around the time her fingers had started to regain their feeling from the short walk inside, she'd decided that she needed this.

Growing up, she didn't remember Kingsford being this busy, even during peak tourist season in the summer. It had been an idyllic, if not a little boring, small town. Now, it seemed to be filled with vacationing families and hipsters working remotely. Bad for her inability to wait in line without rolling her eyes, but good for her bar tips.

She'd never admit to her dad that she was making more bartending than working as a photographer, even during her best months in the city. But no one ever said you'd get paid a lot to do what you love.

Still, it was exciting to finally have a little money in the bank, and even if her current roommate was not ideal, living with only one person was a nice change of pace. She had her own bathroom again, which felt about as close to the height of luxury as she'd come lately. The last time she'd had one, it had been the same bathroom.

Though, if she was going to mention the good, it was also worth pointing out that everything in this town moved so unbelievably slowly. Coffee—better budget an hour. Gym—try and snag one of the machines from the old ladies at your own risk. They'd get up when they were good and ready.

It took twenty minutes for her to get to the front of the line, even though there had only been four people in front of her. Maybe she was running on New York minutes, but she was practically buzzing with unspent energy when she reached the counter.

And the small talk. Yes, it was cold. Yes, she'd seen the beautiful Christmas tree lot next door. No, she didn't know any kids in the holiday pageant. On and on and on the questions happened. At the coffee shop. At the grocery store. At any business that wasn't manned by a self-checkout. Which, unfortunately, was most of them.

Did no one here brood? Was there not a single misanthropic Scrooge in the bunch? Not even a Grinch? They were as much a part of the holiday folklore as the happy, jolly crowd, and, in her opinion, it was a little rude being made so invisible.

Instead, Kingsford had decided to lean hard into the magic of the holiday season. It felt like bright lights had been strung on almost every tree within sight, and they'd placed a giant sleigh in the park near the water. She'd seen more than a few families trying to brave the winter weather to take pictures on it. Idiots.

When she had her flat white in hand, which, again in the sake of fairness, was just as good as she got back in the city, she weaved through the crowd that had swelled in size since she'd arrived and, doing something she never thought would happen in these temperatures, welcomed pushing the door open and getting outside.

Which she regretted immediately. Sometimes, you only learned about all the places sweat hadn't dried yet once you were confronted with below-freezing temperatures. That was one of those facts they didn't teach kids in school, though she did have a flashback of being forced to run the mile in ninety-degree heat on the gravel middle school track and then being forced to go back to class like that was completely normal.

Even after coming back, she hadn't thought much about her childhood here. She'd been, to put it kindly, a late bloomer. Quiet and shy, she'd been more interested in taking photos than talking to people. Which, in retrospect, she admitted made her stick out like a sore thumb.

Layer on confusing, but not concrete, feelings about her sexuality, and it had been a recipe for isolation. Proven by the fact that there wasn't a single person she'd felt the need to inform of her return home.

"Fuck," she muttered, as much about the memories as the cold, her breath visible in an angry little puff in front of her. She rounded her shoulders, as if it would help, and walked the thirty frustrating feet perpendicular to where she needed to go so that she could use the crosswalk instead. There were far too many elderly people who hadn't had their driver's licenses confiscated yet for her to take chances.

She felt her phone vibrate in her pocket, and she shifted her coffee cup to her other hand and pulled it out. Yesterday, she'd sent Sawyer her contact information, and she was waiting to finalize a time to meet with her that week.

Sawyer Kent – 11:22 a.m.
Hey, sorry for the slow response… a little under the weather yesterday. Which you probably knew after seeing us leave on Friday. :) Anyway, I have about 200 pieces from the original store that I want to catalog and put up for sale online. At least a few photos per piece.

Maeve almost dropped her phone on the sidewalk. That was probably weeks of work. She resisted getting too excited until she hammered out details on pricing. People had very different opinions on what high-quality photographs should cost.

Even if she didn't get that sense from Sawyer, it was her responsibility to cover her bases before agreeing to anything.

She'd done this back-and-forth enough to be diplomatic but direct.

Maeve Murphy – 11:25 a.m.
Were you looking for a quote on the whole project or an hourly rate for my time?

Sawyer Kent – 11:26 a.m.
Your choice. I already baked hiring someone into the budget for acquiring the pieces. They'll have a much better chance of

selling online, so I don't want to skimp on the quality of the photography.

There was a second where Maeve thought about doing a little happy dance on the street, but she resisted. She was not the Cindy Lou Who in this story, though it did feel kind of like a Christmas miracle had just fallen into her lap.

She realized she was standing in the middle of the sidewalk when a heavy shopping bag brushed against her jacket, enough that she felt it but not enough to move her. Instead of being annoyed, because she was in far too good of a mood for that, she started walking again, her mind running in overdrive as she tried to craft the perfect response.

It seemed like Sawyer wanted to use her, even if she hadn't seen any of Maeve's previous work. But hey, she wasn't going to bring that up unless Sawyer did.

Hourly was probably best. She may not be in town long enough to finish everything, and honoring whatever commitment she made was important.

Two hundred antiques. Assume three photos per piece. If the space was available, she'd only have to set up the backdrop once.

So in terms of hours, that would be about...

Something fragrant enveloped her senses. More than that, she was *touching* something fragrant. It was so close she was surprised she hadn't snorted a pine needle. Which would have made her laugh if she wasn't so confused.

"What the fuck?" she said, looking up as the pine needles grazed along her face, tickling her cold skin.

Who missed a literal tree standing in front of them? Apparently her.

A head popped around what she now realized was a

Christmas tree from the lot next door. Whoever had purchased it was waiting to lug it across the crosswalk.

"Little ears are all around us. Pageant practice just got out." Because who else would it be except Jonny, a stupid smirk on his face as he eyed Maeve.

She took a step back and barely had time to roll her eyes before another person popped around the opposite side.

"Maeve?" Bianca was dressed like she'd stepped out of a winter fashion catalog, wearing a bright puffy vest with a flannel layered underneath. Her hair cascaded in loose waves down her front, held perfectly in place by a beanie.

And after her trip to the gym, Maeve looked like the swamp monster's first cousin. Maybe it's sibling, but she was trying to be kind to herself. It was the holidays after all.

It could have been worse, she told herself. She'd only gotten awkwardly close to the tree, like she'd wanted to get to know it a little better, as opposed to running straight into it and spilling her worth-the-twenty-minute-wait coffee everywhere.

She shoved her phone back in her pocket and smiled, hoping they could all just pretend this hadn't happened. "Great tree," she said, like she knew anything about them.

From her expert opinion, she could surmise that this one was... green. And really did smell amazing, like an exorbitantly expensive candle someone bought that still only came half as close to capturing the scent she was inhaling now.

"Do you two need a minute?" Jonny asked.

Bianca shot him a confused look and jutted her arm out to keep the tree standing upright. "Why would we need a minute?"

"I meant Maeve and the tree."

A little smile tugged at the edges of Bianca's lips, and Maeve wanted to melt into the pavement like Frosty the Snowman.

She could feel her cheeks start to heat up, surprised at how quickly she could slip back into feeling like the cool kids were taking potshots at her. It wasn't something she'd thought about in a long time, but being back in Kingsford had a way of amplifying a lot of things she'd done her best to push deep down.

And the second Bianca noticed, which Maeve didn't know if she loved or hated, her smile softened and she leaned her tall frame into the tree. "Movie night tomorrow? You can help me decorate this bad boy after it settles."

Great. A pity invite. That was just what Maeve needed. "That's not—"

"Please," Bianca said, taking a step toward her. "I don't want to do it alone, but my mom will have all kinds of ideas about the feng shui of the ornaments. I don't know if I can handle that. Really, you'd be doing me a favor."

Maeve stood up straighter and tried to regroup. "Do I look like the kind of person that does favors for people?" She nodded toward Jonny. "What about him?"

"I have a name, you know."

"He's busy." Bianca's smile was so disarmingly sincere that Maeve felt like she would have followed her anywhere in that moment.

"I don't know…" Maeve stalled. "Monday nights always have the easiest Jeopardy answers."

"You can watch it at my place. Say yes? Please." Bianca's voice was doing this little singsongy thing where it shifted registers, her eyes bright and focused completely on Maeve.

She doubted Bianca had to plead for anything very often, and Maeve found it more than a little compelling. "Sure. I'll help you decorate your tree."

"Is that a eu—"

Bianca was faster than Maeve had given her credit for, her

hand already slapping Jonny's arm when she spoke. "Shut it, Jonny."

When the light changed for probably the third time they'd been standing there, Jonny picked up the tree. "I'm freezing out here. Can we get this back to your house?"

"See you tomorrow," Bianca said with a wave and a smile so warm it could probably melt icicles.

* * *

"So, what's Jonny doing tonight?" Maeve asked as she wove a strand of lights through the tree now situated in Bianca's living room.

"What?" Bianca asked. She'd been… distracted.

Maeve had shown up an hour ago in a distressed tank top that was quickly becoming Bianca's idea of the perfect shirt. Apparently, Maeve had decided it was too hot with the fireplace going to keep her flannel on, and she'd thrown it across the back of Bianca's sofa before getting down to work.

She'd had this look in her eye while she surveyed the tree from every angle, concentrating like what they were doing was the most important thing in the world.

And that was a little hot too.

Popping up from her knees after she tucked the end of the strand of lights toward the outlet at the wall, she gave Bianca a confused look. "I asked what Jonny was doing. Didn't you say yesterday he was busy?"

"Oh, right. He bowls on Monday nights." At least she hadn't been lying about him not being available, which, she'd realized on her way home with the tree, she would have done just to get Maeve to say yes.

A sound of pure, indulgent glee burst out of Maeve's lips. "Shut up. Really?"

Bianca nodded. "One of the guys he works with got him into it. I think he thought he'd meet some lovable bear there, but no such luck yet."

"Tragic," Maeve deadpanned.

"It's a pretty popular weekly hangout. Our dads are both in the league too. It's actually how they met."

"Oh," Maeve said quietly, her posture shifting a little. She wiped her hands on the front of her jeans and walked over to the sofa, leaning against the back of it and crossing her ankles. "I didn't know that."

Bianca was never sure how to tread when talking about Maeve's dad. Her family in general. It was obvious she and Patrick didn't have a great relationship, though neither of them discussed it. They were cordial at work, and Bianca knew Maeve was living with him, but there was nothing that she noticed pointing to any type of real connection between the two of them.

"Yeah, so…" Bianca figured she should just bite the bullet and say exactly what she knew her dad was going to be discussing with Patrick tonight. To be fair, she'd only found out about it a few hours ago when her mom had texted her, so it wasn't like she'd intentionally sat on the information. "My dad loves the holidays, and since the bar was open on Thanksgiving, he's kind of insisting that you and Patrick come to Christmas Eve at our house this year."

There wasn't a lot she'd seen so far that knocked Maeve off her toes, but she looked like Bianca had just told her a meteor was rocketing toward Earth and they only had minutes to live.

"I don't know if that's…" Maeve blew out a breath but didn't finish her sentence.

"We're friends, right?" Bianca took a step closer.

She felt a little twinge of disappointment at how long it took Maeve to respond. "Yeah."

Cuffing Season

"So, I mean... obviously you don't need to talk to me about anything you don't want to, but I'm happy to lend an ear. I've been told I'm a pretty good listener." She gave her most charming smile and stayed silent for a few seconds to really sell it.

Only Maeve didn't say anything, instead choosing to focus on the boxes of ornaments strewn around the living room.

Bianca took another step and then another. When she reached the sofa, she turned around and leaned the same way Maeve was doing, and she bumped their shoulders together. "I can't prove to you what a great listener I am if you don't say anything."

She was never this pushy, but generally, she couldn't get people to shut up around her. Instead, Maeve fidgeted with the rings on her hand, sliding a large, simple silver band around her thumb in a way that seemed to soothe her.

Finally, it seemed like she wasn't going to get an answer. Bianca conceded gracefully to make sure the rest of the night wasn't awkward. "But we can also just decor—"

"Christmas is hard. Being here is hard. Living with my dad is hard. It's all hard. And I know that running back to New York City will stop me from having to think about it, but it won't solve the problems."

That may have been the longest string of thoughts she'd ever heard Maeve verbalize. And boy, did they pack a punch into Bianca's heart.

Instead of worrying about her own anxious thoughts, Bianca did what she would do for anyone else in this situation. She took Maeve's hand and slid it between her own. Squeezing lightly, she met Maeve's impossibly blue eyes. "That's a pretty self-aware thing to realize, though."

The little sound Maeve made before she spoke said more about how she was really feeling than her frustrated words.

But, for whatever reason, she still didn't want to let the sadness shine through the anger. "It's all so fucked. And now it's just the two of us, and it feels doubly fucked."

"Is fucked a... technical term?" Bianca asked, her voice soft, like the one she'd use with a skittish animal at the vet.

She could see the edges of Maeve's lips tilt upward. "Usually it's a verb."

Okay. She did not need that visual right now while she was trying to play the comforting friend.

Squeezing Maeve's hand, she pulled her attention back, sad, blue eyes looking up at her. "Why don't we focus on one thing at a time?"

Maeve let out a little scoff but didn't look away. That was progress. "Well, not to be difficult, but it feels like the Christmas tree lights we picked out of the boxes earlier."

"How so?" Bianca asked, unable to resist moving a little closer. She liked the warmth radiating from Maeve.

"They were all tangled, and I couldn't just get one strand out to start. I had to work on them all together, even though I just wanted to get started putting them on the tree."

Bianca really should have done a better job with that last year, but that wasn't the point.

And she'd watched the situation play out, now wondering if they'd seen it the same way. As if she didn't remember every second of what had taken place after Maeve had arrived, when she'd wrestled with the strings before carefully sitting down and slowly beginning to untangle them.

"You had to start on them all together, but one did come out first. Then you took off your flannel, like you were ready to do battle, and dove right back in to finish the rest." Bianca smiled but tried not to let just how much she remembered that scene show on her face.

Running her free hand through her hair, Maeve sighed.

"Well, yeah, because we needed them. I'd have ended up right in the same boat fifteen minutes later if I didn't finish."

"So maybe look at it like this. It's all tangled now, and feels like you're not making progress, but things will eventually shake out."

"Like the nest of spiders I found in there earlier."

Every atom in Bianca's body snapped to attention until she saw the mirthful look in Maeve's eyes. "You're messing with me, right?"

"Yes, I'm messing with you."

Bianca let out an audible breath. "Oh my god. Please never joke about that again. I hate spiders. And honestly... I have a lot of guilt about it. I love animals, but..." She shuddered. "The creeping and crawling and all the legs. Too many legs." She wondered for a brief second if she sounded insane, but lots of people didn't like things that skittered around.

"I'll be sure to call the vet's office on Monday and inform them of this sacrilege."

"Being single is all fun and games until there's no one to kill the spiders."

"Maybe that's the truth of what we all want: someone to kill the spiders." It was a "blink and you miss it" moment, when Maeve's focus dropped to Bianca's lips and then quickly shifted upward, only this time she didn't make eye contact.

And it hadn't been what Maeve was implying with the statement, at least that was what Bianca needed to tell herself, but she became acutely aware of how they were still holding hands, their bodies now leaning inward so their knees and thighs were touching.

Something heady sluiced through her veins, a feeling that was unhelpful to name, especially given the current context of their conversation. She tried to put a leash on it, clearing her throat and walking out of whatever she'd accidentally stumbled into. "So Christmas. You'll come?"

Because she wanted Maeve there. Not just for Maeve... but for herself. She could at least admit that.

Bianca hadn't realized she was holding her breath until Maeve's surprisingly soft voice floated between them, devoid of its usual sharp edge. "Sure. I'll come."

Chapter Eight

After whatever moment she'd shared with Bianca the night before, they'd been texting steadily. It had started when Bianca insisted Maeve let her know when she made it home, even though it had only been a five-minute drive.

She could still hear Bianca's voice, full of worry when she'd mentioned the black ice at least three times as she'd walked Maeve to the door.

And then Maeve, in her typical foot-in-mouth fashion, had made a horrible joke about being well-informed on the dangers of car accidents, and she'd thought Bianca was going to start crying in the living room.

It could have easily been the end of the newest step they'd found themselves climbing as friends, but it wasn't.

Maeve was thankful for that. Maybe more than she wanted to let on, she realized, after their tenth exchange of the morning. If she'd already agreed to Christmas at Bianca's house with her dad in tow, how much harm could having someone to text with really cause?

And really, it was Bianca's fault for picking things up again this morning. She'd texted her a picture of the fully decorated Christmas tree at seven a.m. Only that wasn't what had caught Maeve's attention. She's been struck a little speechless by Bianca, sitting on her sofa, a coffee cup in hand as she took the photo with the tree lit up brightly in the background.

Obviously she'd pushed away the feeling of what a nice text that had been to wake up to, instead asking what kind of lunatic actually had time to sit and ease into their morning, which had led to a steady stream of conversation through her morning about all the little things about Bianca she hadn't known.

That she always made an egg-white omelette with ricotta before work. How she made sure to get to the vet's office early to be as prepared for the day as possible. Maeve had laughed and rolled her eyes, even though no one could see, when Bianca admitted that she usually laid out her outfit for the next day the night before.

It was hard to believe that a person like Bianca existed. Down-to-earth. Striking. Didn't seem to have any serious baggage that made her lash out.

Not that Maeve knew anything about that...

And yet here she was. In Kingsford of all places.

The irony did not escape Maeve.

She was lurking around the gym, waiting to get the last machine she needed before she could leave, when she shot off another text.

Maeve Murphy – 10:09 a.m.

I'd take a picture but that's rude. So, to paint the scene for you: there are a gaggle of women in their sixties and seventies who appear to be doing synchronized stretching.

. . .

Bianca's response came back almost immediately.

Bianca Rossi – 10:10 a.m.
Are you trying to make some more friends? Just going from beginner to expert level in the blink of an eye.

Maeve Murphy – 10:11 a.m.
I have... a friend. :) Zero to one is literally an infinite improvement. I figure I should suss this whole thing out before I go too crazy with it.

Bianca Rossi – 10:12 a.m.
We can always rope in Jonny for you to practice on.

Maeve Murphy – 10:13 a.m.
You really had to bring down my good time like that?

Bianca Rossi – 10:13 a.m.
He's great, I swear.

Why Bianca cared if Maeve liked her friends was beyond her. But another text—well, multiple texts—followed soon after.

Bianca Rossi – 10:13 a.m.

When I moved to Kingsford it was nice to have someone who didn't want anything from me.

Bianca Rossi – 10:13 a.m.
I mean... not to sound cocky. Not at all. Sorry if it came off that way. Just...

Bianca Rossi – 10:13 a.m.
You get it, right? You must get it.

Right, the whole model-level attractive thing Bianca had going, though Maeve couldn't understand why Bianca thought she'd get it except in anything other than an abstract way. Women could be catty and men could be aggressive.

The last few times they'd seen one another, Maeve had almost forgotten about how ridiculously good-looking Bianca was. Bianca would do something like waddle across her living room like a duck to make a point or, like she'd done last week, turn toward Maeve behind the bar with two straws stuck in her mouth like walrus tusks.

Her love for animals, with the exception of spiders, seemed to extend to imitating them.

Even in just a few weeks of friendship, she'd become this fully realized person to Maeve, with her quirks and habits. Her ridiculous affinity for cheesy holiday movies was even starting to grow on Maeve. They'd watched them instead of Jeopardy last night—though she'd never admit it to another living soul.

Yet again, reinforcing a point that shouldn't even need to be reinforced, it proved just how firmly in the camp of "friends and nothing else" their relationship was.

And it needed to stay there.

Maeve Murphy – 10:15 a.m.
What I don't get is your horrible taste in friends. Jonny? Me? Are you trying to assemble some misfit island of toys?

Bianca Rossi – 10:15 a.m.
Easy is no fun :)

Maeve almost responded with just how fun easy could be sometimes, but she stopped herself.

"Machine's free," a gravelly voice said from beside her.

She jumped, fumbling with her phone but managing not to drop it. When she was finally confident she wasn't going to break the most expensive thing she owned besides her camera equipment, she looked up and met the stare of one of the gym regulars.

Blowing out a breath, she stood up a little straighter under the woman's critical stare. "Thanks."

"Kids these days. Always on their phones." Maeve was pushing thirty, but sure. The woman saying it had to be at least in her seventies, so that was probably a blanket word for anyone who didn't have grandkids yet.

Still, it annoyed her. "It's the last machine I needed today," Maeve said before she looked the woman up and down and added, "I guess you needed a little more time between sets than I was expecting."

Honestly, though, she didn't know if she could take this woman in a fight. She was older by decades, but there was a fire in her eyes that made Maeve think twice about her words.

Too bad she was thinking about them after she'd already said them. Story of her life.

The woman was fit in a way that made her seem more ageless than anything, reminding Maeve of her own wiry frame. With silver hair that was just long enough to pull back into a ponytail, she wore what looked like a fairly expensive—and coordinated—workout outfit.

Maeve shouldn't have talked shit. She'd kill to look like this woman in forty years.

But she wasn't really good at apologizing. "Okay, well... Guess I'll go use the machine then."

When the woman followed her over, trailing a step behind, Maeve gave her a curious look but didn't say anything, assuming she'd forgotten something. After she sat down on the seat and adjusted the weight minimally, the woman was still standing next to her.

"Can I help you with something?"

The woman smirked. "Let's see what you've got, kid. Maybe you can teach me a thing or two about resting between sets."

* * *

Maeve Murphy – 10:35 a.m.
 <<photo>>
 This is Shirley. I don't know if we're going to be best friends or mortal enemies, but apparently she knows her way around a chest press machine.

It took Bianca a few minutes before she could check her phone after it vibrated. She hoped it was Maeve, who'd gone radio silent after Bianca's last comment about not liking things easy.

Bianca wasn't really used to having to woo people, friends or otherwise, and it was making her feel more than a little unsteady.

Maeve was hard to read. Add in her sarcasm and seemingly never-ending love of dark humor, and Bianca was constantly wondering what would pop out of Maeve's mouth.

And then there were those sparing moments of vulnerability, like she'd shown Bianca last night. It had felt good—really good—to be the person that Maeve had let in.

Instead of dwelling on that, though, she responded. The banter made things easier, provided they didn't veer into dangerous territory.

Bianca Rossi – 10:42 a.m.
You did something to piss her off, didn't you?

Maeve Murphy – 11:00 a.m.
Sorry, I was in the shower. And she started it!

Bianca was doing a lot to not go down the rabbit hole of that visual when Kelly's voice pulled her attention.

"I know that look. Who's got you smiling like that?" Kelly was leaning on the counter in front of Bianca's desk like she'd been there for a little while and Bianca hadn't even noticed. And she probably hadn't, which wasn't her usual style.

"No, it's not like that. I'm pretty sure Maeve got in a fight with a lady quite a bit older than her at the gym, but it seems like they're becoming friends." She tried but failed to dim her smile as she recounted the situation.

"Seems like Maeve's making all kinds of *friends*," Kelly said, the implication clear in her words.

"She's..." Bianca didn't want to give the impression that something was going on that wasn't. Because really, they were just friends. Who hung out. And had started having deep conversations about complicated emotions. And maybe Bianca looked forward to seeing her. A lot. And texting with her all morning had made the day breeze by and given her a renewed sense of excitement for all the mundane things in her day-to-day, as she was curious to see what Maeve thought about them. Like friends did. "She's coming around a little bit. Bummer that she's going to leave so soon, but it's been nice."

Kelly nodded and glanced at the clock on the wall before settling her focus back to Bianca. "Interesting. That's what Sawyer said too."

That made Bianca's ears perk up. "Why would Sawyer know?"

The conspiratorial smile that Kelly gave her made it clear to Bianca that she'd failed some sort of test with her quick and intense interest. She'd always been curious! So sue her!

"Maeve's going to photograph some of the pieces Sawyer bought from the other shop. Only she couldn't commit to the full project, so they're doing it hourly for as long as Maeve's in town. Hopefully she'll get through most of them."

Oh... She was surprised that Maeve hadn't mentioned it. She pushed away the little sting of hurt.

Kelly, though, was like some sort of wizard, her eyes tracking over Bianca's face as her own settled into understanding. "They just officially worked it out today. The news is hot off the press."

"Well, good for Maeve." And really, her own niggling confusion aside, she meant it. It was a good opportunity and might make Maeve's time in town a little happier, doing something she loved.

"Anyway," Kelly said, nodding over her shoulder. "Dennis and his owner just came in. He's getting his Lyme booster, so it should be a quick appointment. I'll be back in a minute to grab him."

In all her distraction texting Maeve this morning, she hadn't even noticed his name on the schedule. Still, she gave him a bright smile when Kelly moved away so that he could step up to the counter.

"Hey, Jack." She leaned over the counter and nodded at the well-behaved dog. "Dennis."

Jack's smile was... charming, for lack of a better word. Like he was focused on you fully and having a great time while he did it. It didn't have the same lop-sided lean Maeve's did. She always seemed two steps ahead of any conversation, as long as it wasn't about emotions, waiting for you to catch up on whatever joke she was leading you into.

"Kelly should be out for Dennis in just a minute."

"Thanks." Jack remained standing at the counter, like he was gearing himself up for something. Bianca had seen that look before. "So I was wondering..."

Honestly, she felt for the guy. Being the person who asked people on dates was hard. Men got a lot of really deserved shit for a multitude of everything, but facing rejection, regardless of a pedestal of privilege, was still not fun.

As she considered the situation, the reality hit Bianca that she didn't know if she would reject him. He had a well-behaved dog. Was handsome with his clean-shaven face and well-styled hair. Knew how to function at bars. She'd already given him a pass on cuffing season since he was new to town. He was exactly the type of person she'd told herself she'd been looking for.

And it all had to start somewhere.

Maybe she'd learn the other stuff and like that too. Did he untangle Christmas lights like a demonic cat? Was he insistent that apple cider should always be chilled and never hot? Did he run his hands through his hair whenever he was stalling for time?

Okay, that had gotten off track.

She looked back up to meet Jack's curious stare, realizing the moment had gotten away from her. Because it was the person standing in front of her that she should have been focusing on, not anyone else.

"I take it that's a no?" He sounded disappointed, though she hadn't been listening and could only assume what he'd asked.

Shaking her head, she pretended to organize a few papers next to her computer. Their purpose escaped her just then. "I'm sorry. Busy morning. Can you repeat whatever you said?"

To his credit, Jack looked more sheepish than anything. He put his hands palms down on the counter and relaxed his shoulders. "Yeah, I know it's probably not the best look to ask someone out at their place of work, but that's the only place I seem to see you. So I was asking if you'd be interested in meeting up in a place that's not related to where you work."

Bianca studied him. He seemed sincere. The request wasn't too pushy. And how often was there someone new in her life that kept popping up, almost like a sign?

Well, she wasn't going to pick that one apart.

"So like… a date?" She'd found it best to be overly communicative about these situations from the start. Too many vague conversations with men had led to a need for very clear boundary setting on her part. Honestly, it was exhausting.

Jack nodded. "In the sake of full disclosure, I would like for it to be a date."

It all had to start somewhere, she reminded herself. And if she wanted the chance to find it, she had to be willing to take the leap.

"Sure, a date sounds great."

Chapter Nine

It was the week before Christmas, and Maeve wondered if the city of Kingsford would outpace the supply at which they could restock alcohol. The holidays seemed to make people want to drink their faces off in dimly lit bars. They were busy almost every night they were open, and with eight days to go until Christmas, hearing "Jingle Bells" again in ten years would still be too soon.

She'd wondered more than a few times if the city had brokered some sort of deal to bring itself as close to Santa's Village as possible for the tourism dollars. Every tree was decorated. Every store was playing Christmas music. She'd seen an elf walking around earlier that day. An elf!

Still, it was difficult to be her usual curmudgeonly self, especially after receiving her first payment from Sawyer, who'd been true to her word that, during their project together, quality was more of a focus than cost.

Today, she'd spent four hours at the antique shop before coming to the bar. It was a schedule that had been working so far, spending a few hours each morning before her evening shift to catalog the items. This had been her third day, and she was only through about ten percent of the pieces.

Sawyer would get really excited about the shots Maeve was taking and then ask her to take more and from a variety of different angles. And what Maeve hadn't anticipated was that for some of the more complicated antiques, they'd need to take exterior photos and then Sawyer would do some sort of magic where she took pieces apart until the internal mechanisms were visible.

It was a slow process, but one Maeve found she was quite enjoying. Sawyer was easy to be around. They were silent a lot of the time, except when Sawyer grew excited about something and started talking a mile a minute about some sort of mechanical aspect. The bigger machines—which it was clear were Sawyer's babies—took far longer to work through given their complexity.

She hadn't understood all the photographic fanfare, but it had become a bit clearer when Sawyer explained that not only were they photographing them for sale, but that it was also a necessary part of insurance inventorying and presale guarantees that all the parts were accounted for and in working order.

She was liking her current day-to-day routine. Wake up. Text with Bianca. Gym. Head to the antique shop. Finish her day working at the bar. They closed at eleven on weeknights, so though she didn't have a lot of energy to spare, it wasn't like she was running on fumes.

She liked being busy. It kept her mind occupied, and it calmed the restlessness usually present in her anxiously wired body. Not that she'd admit it, but she'd been sleeping better this week than she had in years.

And the whole texting with Bianca thing was kind of nice. She couldn't remember the last time that someone had cared about her comings and goings. She couldn't really remember the last time she'd cared about her own except to make sure she didn't miss a job. Now she was seeing things through a different lens.

On Wednesday, she'd texted Bianca a photo of her avocado toast, which she ate almost every morning for breakfast. People could say what they wanted about millennials, but she was poor because of crippling school debt and hyperinflated rent prices. Avocados were not the thing that was going to bring her financial future to its knees.

After she'd seen Shirley at the gym on Thursday, she'd excitedly texted Bianca that they'd both casually but without much fanfare agreed to maybe sometimes come to the gym at a similar time. It was perfect.

As she shook what had to be her hundredth cocktail of the night, she tried to pinpoint the feeling that had been buzzing restlessly through her veins the last few days. It was something that made her keyed up but also left her feeling settled. She hadn't managed to place it, mostly because she didn't know if she'd ever felt it before.

It wasn't anticipation, which was headier and made her want to careen toward whatever was causing that sensation. To call it excitement simplified it too much and cut off the soft edges that made her feel a little bit like she was in a dream.

What was it then?

She poured the whiskey sour into the chilled cocktail glass and added a few drops of bitters for a little design touch. Honestly, she wondered what her dad had been passing off as a cocktail program before she'd arrived.

When she'd moved to the city, picking up a bartending gig had made her want to die a little, since it was exactly what she told herself she'd been leaving behind in Kingsford. But she'd never been too proud to do what needed to be done, and once she'd gotten a few more years of experience, there were always

Cuffing Season

last-minute shifts she could pick up when photography jobs were slow.

Carefully, she placed the glass in front of the customer and gave them a quick smile before walking back to her station and starting in on the dozen tickets waiting for her.

When she looked up, Bianca was looking right at her. Bianca had been running a few minutes late that night, so they hadn't had a chance to talk much before the rush had started. Bianca smiled and picked up a few lemons, pretending to juggle them but failing miserably before she dropped them back on the bar, gave Maeve a thumbs-up, and went back to work at her station.

The paper crumpled between her fingers when it hit her. Optimism. That's what she was feeling. She was hopeful about her future, confident that it would work out, even if she didn't know exactly what it entailed. And she couldn't remember the last time she'd felt that way.

There had been moments over the years. When she'd landed the freelance gig with the media company and her schedule became a little more consistent. After she'd been living at her last apartment for a few months and realized she'd actually ended up with mildly functional adults as roommates.

But they didn't quite touch how she felt now. Because she'd still been scraping and scrambling, barely on solid footing before she was already reaching for the next rung while also waiting for the bottom to drop out underneath her.

If she wanted—if this made her happy—she could continue to do it. She could work at her dad's bar. Pick up photography jobs. Build a... friendship... with Bianca. And even if she didn't do those things, they'd still be here if she needed them.

For the first time, a little pang of sadness hit her at the thought of leaving Kingsford. After all, what was really waiting for her? Lovers that had moved on. Photography, while her true passion, had become a thing she did to make money. She couldn't remember the last time she'd taken photos for herself, because she wanted to capture something about the world.

She could tell herself that it had been coming back that was changing things, but she knew that would be a lie. Because she hadn't started feeling this way until about a month ago, when she'd started to know Bianca better and her days had become a little more exciting.

Sneaking another glance, she watched as Bianca laughed with a customer as she poured their beer perfectly from the tap and placed it on the coaster in front of them. She really was a marvel. Hiding out—no, she was *choosing* to live—in Kingsford of all places.

If the Hudson River had sirens, Bianca was definitely one, luring Maeve back to its rocky shores and making her wonder if crashing her metaphorical boat here wouldn't be the worst thing in the world. Only Bianca's song was a text notification, similar to one she'd gotten this morning, alerting her to pictures of freshly baked cookies and decorated Christmas trees to convince Maeve to join her for another holiday movie marathon.

Which she'd said yes to immediately because she was a glutton for punishment. But they had a good thing going, and if it made her happier in the here and now, it couldn't be worse than how she'd felt a few months ago.

So even if a twinge of optimism about more than just her professional life was starting to take root, she didn't have the strength to shut it down.

* * *

Bianca hadn't stopped moving in hours. When one seat opened, someone else slotted in to take it. The tables on the

Cuffing Season

other side of the bar also remained full, seated as soon as they were cleared from the previous customers. It was like watching one of those festive miniature train sets that just kept going around and around and around. The train wasn't going to stop until someone turned it off.

Which was in a little over an hour. She could make it. At least they'd just stopped serving food. Though that actually wasn't great for her since it meant the people left would only be drinking.

She flexed her hands against the bar. She couldn't remember the last time her forearms had been this sore. If she felt like this, she wondered how bad Maeve must be feeling. Working at a job this physically demanding five nights a week had to be difficult. Maybe not for Maeve, though, Bianca thought as she snuck a glance at the woman working fifteen feet away.

Maeve was lithe but compact, like a wiry Energizer Bunny. She was always moving, always restless, it seemed. Even now, she was shaking a cocktail with her right hand while she loaded the dishwasher with her left. The longest she'd ever seen Maeve sit still was when they'd watched movies, and even then, though she seemed to manage to calm her body, Bianca could tell her mind was moving a mile a minute.

There was something about Maeve that reminded her a little of a feral kitten. Skittish. Brave. Adorable. Though she'd never mention that last one to Maeve. She didn't get the sense that would be an adjective she'd like to be used to describe herself. But with her tousled blonde hair and blue eyes—and that dimple that didn't often come out—she could pass for a very misanthropic angel.

The thought made Bianca smile as she closed out a check and handed it over to the customer. At least she had the rest of the weekend to look forward to, even if it was a shame Maeve had to work Saturday and Sunday nights. It might be fun to go out together, to see Maeve let loose and have some fun outside of their normally structured hangouts or when they saw one another at work.

But that wasn't going to be possible, and then Maeve was leaving. So... maybe she'd see if Maeve wanted to have a fun night on a Monday when she didn't have to work the next day. Bianca would regret her decision on Tuesday morning, but it would be worth it.

She smiled and made a mental note to bring it up with Maeve when they closed down the bar.

On autopilot, she'd already grabbed the receipt from the customer who'd just left, someone else sliding into the seat. She put a coaster down in front of them and flashed her finger up to indicate she'd be with them in a minute. Her water bottle was tucked below the bar, and she grabbed it before turning toward the back bar area and taking a few hearty gulps.

She was turning around when she saw them, stopping mid-step before forcing herself to keep moving. Maeve was near her drink station, leaning forward with her forearms resting on the bar. The woman she was talking to was unmistakably the person Bianca had seen in the alley a month ago. She was definitely attractive, and she seemed like Maeve's style. A little chic, a little grunge, with dark, dyed hair cut into an asymmetrical bob and a full tattoo sleeve running up one of her exposed arms. She hadn't looked nearly as intimidating when Maeve had had her pressed up against the brick wall, like she was a putty puppy dog in her hands.

What was with Bianca comparing people to animals tonight?

Well, good for Maeve. She deserved to have some fun. That was what Bianca told herself, even as the unmistakable feeling of jealousy flowed through her. Because she could still remember the discordant sound that woman had made into the otherwise silent night air, with Maeve up against her, cold fingers pushing into hot skin.

So yeah, Bianca was a little jealous. Because it had been a long time since she'd been touched like that. Maybe she'd never been touched like that. Not by someone like Maeve who always seemed ready to catch fire.

The clandestine nature of their meeting had probably heightened the sensations, but she had no doubt that Maeve was good at whatever she set her mind to. And even if Maeve hadn't said anything about it at the time, the woman's heavily lidded stare and complete inability to snap out of the moment, even after she'd been caught, said a lot more than words could.

So really, Bianca was mostly surprised it had taken her so long to come back.

And when the woman scribbled on a small scrap of paper and pushed it in Maeve's direction, with an indisputably flirty smile to match the hunger in her eyes, Bianca felt like she'd watched the train complete its loop on the track, ready to start again.

*** * ***

Bianca was acting weird. That was the only way Maeve could describe it. She was almost too chipper as they closed down the bar, finally coaxing the last stragglers out well after last call.

When it was just the two of them, Bianca turned to her, voice a little too loud for their close proximity, and said, "So movie night on Monday?"

Someone needed to secretly switch that woman to decaf or something.

Maeve nodded and continued wiping down the bar, trying

to figure out Bianca's deal. "Sure. Monday movie night. Wouldn't miss it."

Bianca clasped her hands together and rocked forward on the tips of her toes before standing still again. "I have a date tomorrow. And seems like you may have a date later tonight. So it seems like we'll have date stories to compare."

Maeve frowned. She had no intention of doing anything with that woman's number. Beth, whose name she now knew, came to town periodically on business as a pharmaceutical rep. This was her last trip of the year, and yes, she'd maybe asked if Maeve wanted to meet back at her hotel later. And yes, maybe Maeve had seriously considered it. But she was tired. More than that, she didn't think scratching that itch would really help all that much in the grand scheme of things. Which was unlike her, but her not feeling burnt-out was only mitigated by not adding too much fuel to the fire. Staying up all night Friday and coming into work Saturday was not going to help her push through another grueling shift.

God, just thinking that made her feel old.

But the more pressing piece of the conversation that Maeve was trying not to think about either was that Bianca apparently had a date.

"Breaking your cuffing season rule?" Maeve asked, trying to keep her voice light. Maybe it made her a bad friend, but she had no interest in discussing Bianca's date when they hung out on Monday.

Bianca's face flushed. "He's new in town, so I felt like the normal rules didn't apply."

"Because people new to town don't like to cuff?"

"I'm not sure it's used as a verb like that."

"It's a made-up word. I'm pretty sure it can be used however I want." She knew she hadn't managed to slice the slight edge from her voice, and when Bianca's face fell, Maeve felt like she'd just kicked a puppy. Gesturing between them, she quickly added, "But I'm sure that..."

"Jack," Bianca supplied.

"Yes, I'm sure Jack is a lovely person and you will have the chance to live out a Hallmark holiday movie with the mysterious outsider who's new in town." Not exactly her best work, but Rome wasn't built in a day.

Bianca looked skeptical, but she unclasped her hands and picked up her bar towel again. "It's just a first date. I try not to get very invested in them because most don't lead to second dates."

"Fair, but you can't have a second date without a first date, right? Seems like a necessary evil." Was this helping? Maeve didn't know. She'd never really had the kind of friends who chatted about their love lives.

"That's true..."

Saying her next words killed Maeve a little inside, but she tried to put on a brave face. "Great. Well, I hope you have a good time tomorrow night."

And for once in her life, she was thrilled that tomorrow she'd probably be so busy she'd barely have time to think.

Chapter Ten

Jonny Boy – 5:52 p.m.
Is your girlfriend there yet? Does your new boyfriend know you already have a girlfriend? It's very modern of you.

It was Monday night, and Bianca was flitting around her kitchen, cooking dinner for her and Maeve, who would be arriving in just a few minutes. Maeve probably ate an inordinate amount of pasta working at the bar so often, so Bianca had decided to make chicken noodle soup with a baguette she'd grabbed from the grocery store on her way home from work. Simple and hearty, the perfect lounging food for a cold night tucked in front of the TV watching movies.

Jonny Boy – 5:53 p.m.
???

. . .

Bianca Rossi – 5:53 p.m.
   Shut it.

That's not what was going on. But let her try and explain that to Jonny. He'd been utterly delighted when they'd met up on Sunday to find out that Bianca had gone on a date. He'd usually have been her first text after something like that happened, but she'd waited until after she and Jack had had drinks to tell him.

And she couldn't really explain why.

So far, Jack was checking all the boxes. Not in the "plucked from a Hallmark movie" way Maeve had implied on Friday, but in the way that meant he at least mildly had his shit together and was a good conversationalist.

He'd gotten his dog, Dennis, from a rescue. He had good table manners, which she'd found out when they'd decided to have dinner after their first drink. His family was back in Georgia, but he'd been excited to advance his career and wanted to give Kingsford a shot.

Everything about meeting him felt, though Bianca would never admit it to Maeve, like it was a little bit movie-esque. All they were missing was a meet-cute where Dennis had stolen her ice cream cone or something and she'd chased him across a park. Too bad it was the dead of winter and she wouldn't be caught dead outside right now unless it was under duress. Or to catch Maeve making out with women against buildings.

Ugh. She needed to stop thinking about that.

But, with the woman reappearing on Friday, it had popped into Bianca's mind more than a few times over the weekend. And then she'd thought about it again when she wondered how Maeve's Friday night had gone. Possibly Saturday, too, if Friday had gone well.

   . . .

***Jonny Boy** – 5:55 p.m.*
 That's so rude. Does your girlfriend know about your date?

***Bianca Rossi** – 5:56 p.m.*
 Yes. I'm muting your notifications now.

Bianca realized the moment she responded that she hadn't corrected Jonny's comment about Maeve being her girlfriend. Maybe because, and it was something she was slightly willing to admit to herself at this point, she didn't mind the sound of it.

Life was so unfair sometimes.

A minute before six, her doorbell rang. She headed through the doorway that connected the kitchen and the living room, crossing the hardwood floor quickly to open the door. It was below freezing out, and she knew that Maeve hated the cold just as much as she did.

"Come in," she said, already stepping to the side as a whoosh of wind and flurries swept through the entry.

Maeve pulled her beanie off her head slowly, the tips of her ears, nose, and cheeks all a bright pink. "Fuck, it's cold."

"You say that like you're still surprised at this point." Bianca moved to take Maeve's coat, but she hadn't eased out of it yet. "So cold you're planning to keep your jacket on?"

An extra little flush of color bloomed on Maeve's cheeks. "I may have overdone it at the gym a little bit yesterday. I think I tweaked something in my shoulder, and working last night didn't really help it at all."

"Oh god, Maeve. We could have rescheduled if you weren't feeling well."

Maeve waved her hand limply, not raising it as much as she normally would. "I'm fine, I promise. It'll be better tomorrow."

Bianca didn't exactly believe her, but Maeve was already in her entryway, so it wasn't like she could send her home now. "Okay. Why don't you take off your coat at whatever speed you're operating at right now, and I'll grab a heating pad to put on your shoulder."

Maeve nodded without putting up a fight. Apparently, even the most feral kittens could be coaxed with the promise of warmth.

"Give me a minute. When your coat's off, you can go sit on the sofa. I made chicken noodle soup, and I'll bring you a bowl."

"Wow. This is really a full-service evening. I feel like you're either the world's most hospitable person, or we're gearing up to watch the cheesiest holiday movie ever made." Maeve rolled her eyes good-naturedly and began slowly taking off her coat.

"Guess we'll find out."

It only took Bianca about thirty seconds to grab the heating pad, since she slept with it sometimes in the colder months. She plugged it into the outlet next to where Maeve was seated and looked down at Maeve, who was wearing a button-down flannel.

"This couch is so comfy."

"They're supposed to be comfy." Bianca pointed at Maeve's shirt. "Can you get the pad underneath it, or do you need help?"

"Is taking my shirt off an option?" Bianca's eyes went a little wide before Maeve clarified quickly, "I have another shirt under it. Don't worry. I'm not asking to hang out in your living room in a bra. Well, honestly... I'm not wearing a bra, but I do have a tank top on. Promise."

Oh, okay. Sure. Why not. Because nothing bad could come from this. Maeve was practically broken right now. It wasn't like the idea of stripping in the hopes of getting lucky was on her mind.

Bianca realized Maeve was still staring at her, unmoving. Probably because Bianca hadn't actually answered. "That's totally fine. I used to be around naked women all the time." Now it was Maeve's turn for her eyes to bug out of her head a little bit, comically so. "Oh god. What I meant was modeling. Lots of shared fitting rooms, and well, for fashion supposedly being about clothing, a lot of modeling doesn't involve a heck of a lot of it."

Maeve let out a snort laugh followed by a grunt as the pain in her shoulder made her still her body quickly.

Bianca felt like it was best to back out of the room now, worried she'd say something even more stupid if she stayed any longer. "I'll grab soup. You work on getting your shirt off." Well, distance hadn't really helped her mouth, which currently had a mind of its own.

She took her time ladling the soup into two bowls and cutting off chunks of bread, trying to give Maeve a little privacy to get down to her tank top. And not that there was anything sexual about it, given Maeve's current state, but the idea of watching her undress for any reason caused Bianca's stomach to flip a little more aggressively than she wanted to acknowledge right now.

After she waited another minute for good measure, she took the soup, bread, and utensils into the living room on a tray and placed it on the coffee table. Maeve had managed to get her shirt off. The heating pad was between her back and the sofa, and she was leaning against it to keep the pad in place.

"Comfy enough?" Bianca asked as she picked up a bowl and handed it to Maeve.

"This is perfect. Thank you." Her voice was smaller than normal as she accepted the soup and blew on it gently.

Cuffing Season

And that caused another little flip in Bianca's stomach for wholly different reasons. The Maeve in front of her looked tired and in pain. And like, until this exact moment, she'd assumed she'd have to shoulder that burden alone.

But she wasn't alone, and Bianca didn't ever want her to think that. She put on a movie while they ate dinner, a new holiday one that had premiered on Friday night when she'd been working. She snuck glances at Maeve, who ate gingerly but finished the entire bowl. When she was done, Bianca wordlessly took the bowl from her hands and put it back on the coffee table.

Maeve sighed contentedly. "Thank you. Now my outsides and my insides are warm. Is this what heaven feels like?"

"If it was heaven, you'd be dead right now."

"Then I'd die happy," Maeve said, a look of sheer contentment on her face that Bianca didn't know if she'd ever seen the other woman wear.

"Wanna ratchet this happiness knob up to eleven?" What she was on the verge of proposing was a bad, terrible, inarguably insane idea for so many reasons. Which meant she pretty much couldn't stop herself.

Maeve lifted a sculpted eyebrow a few shades darker than her hair and tilted her body toward Bianca. "How so?"

"Sit on the floor." Bianca shifted her knees open wider and pointed to the rugged floor between her legs. "I promise, I know what I'm doing."

"And how do I know that?" Maeve asked, but she was already scooting forward on the sofa to lift herself up with her legs.

Bianca rolled her eyes but stopped short when Maeve braced the hand attached to her good arm on Bianca's thigh to lower herself down to the ground. It seemed like Maeve didn't really care about her answer, which was perfect because she was finding it a little difficult to form words as Maeve situated herself cross-legged on the floor in front of Bianca.

"Is this okay?" Maeve asked after Bianca had been silent for thirty seconds, distracted by the lingering feeling of Maeve's palm like a brand on her jogger-clad thigh. "Or was this just some elaborate ruse so you could stretch out on the sofa?"

When her hands met Maeve's exposed shoulder, there was the briefest moment where Maeve's back tensed, but she relaxed against Bianca's fingertips and let out a soft sigh.

Whatever Bianca had been expecting, it wasn't the softness of Maeve's skin, like her fingers were gliding through water with her first, tentative touches. She started by pushing her thumb gently against Maeve's shoulder while her left hand came up to stabilize Maeve's other side and hold her in place.

Maeve stayed completely still. Not a bounce or a movement or a fidget. Like a statue, Maeve allowed Bianca's fingers to wander, and she used an intentionally soft pressure at first to gauge the tenderness of the hurt area.

"How's that feeling?" Bianca asked, surprised when her voice barely came out as a whisper, like she was worried she'd startle Maeve, or possibly herself, out of this moment.

"So good." Maeve's voice was a little breathless, a little raw, and it caused a pleasurable ache to sprawl across Bianca's body.

Because god... imagining hearing that tone in other contexts made Bianca's face flush with heat.

Emboldened by Maeve's encouraging words, she pressed her fingers a little more insistently. It was indulgent—she knew that—the way she splayed her hand across Maeve's exposed skin and let the heat soak into her fingertips.

Maeve sighed, and, as another little piece of her resolve chipped away, Bianca shifted her thumb against the tender area and started working into it in small, focused circles.

This—whatever Bianca was doing right now—didn't feel

like anything close to the dozens of massages she and her friends had given one another after hard modelling gigs, when they'd had to stand in heels for hours or in uncomfortable poses that no human body should be able to contort into. This felt intimate. And Bianca liked it a lot. She liked how Maeve's body was firm yet pliant. And she liked the little freckles dotting across Maeve's shoulder blades. For a euphoria-induced second, because of how good this felt and how good other things would probably feel, too, Bianca considered shifting forward and placing a light kiss on one.

God, she needed to get a grip. They'd managed to find some level of friendship—at Bianca's insistence, no less—and here she was like some horny teenager who'd never touched someone before.

She tried to focus on how to make Maeve feel better instead of how good touching her made her feel. That wasn't working especially well either. Thinking about Maeve deriving any sort of pleasure from Bianca's hands on her set her mind whirring again with a world of possibility.

Bianca was trying to get herself under control when Maeve made this... sound. The best way to describe it was like a sound of release. Quiet, but from the back of her throat, like something inside of her had loosened and she was exhaling more than just air.

All Bianca wanted at this moment was to taste the skin she'd been touching, her jaw tight at the thought. But it wouldn't be right. Or fair.

Bianca was the one who'd pushed them to be friends. And Bianca was the one who'd wanted them to hang out together outside of work. And, yet again, point to Bianca for orchestrating a situation where Maeve was between her legs.

"Feel better?" Bianca asked, channeling a restraint she didn't know she possessed as she pulled her hands away.

Whatever she was feeling, she had no idea if Maeve was feeling the same way.

* * *

Maeve had never been touched like that before. Sweetly. Softly. Almost reverently. She had been touched with purpose by women before, but never like this, when the goal was to soothe and comfort.

She leaned her back against the sofa when Bianca removed her hands, immediately missing the contact.

She cleared her throat, unsure how her voice would sound. Maybe a little low with want. Maybe a lot squeaky with the probable embarrassment at her body betraying her. Because Bianca Rossi had magical fingers. Long and strong, they'd pushed against the tenderness until it felt like Maeve could feel her inside of her, which was... not helpful.

Staying still had been the hardest thing she'd maybe ever done, when all she'd wanted was to change how she was sitting to ease the friction building between her legs.

Thank god they hadn't been looking at one another while this was going on. Maeve didn't know what she would have done if Bianca's green eyes had been looking at her with the same intensity flowing through her fingertips.

"Here, let me help you up," Bianca said, scrambling around Maeve on the sofa until she stood next to her.

Bianca's toes were painted a festive green, which shouldn't have surprised Maeve at all but somehow still did. She hadn't noticed it when she'd arrived, when she was just trying to breathe through her nose and will away the pain.

Now, though, with the pain manageable after a heating pad, a delicious dinner, and a massage that made her feel indecent, she was starting to take notice of Bianca in a way she'd been working so hard to quell.

Her stomach twisted when Bianca extended her hand to Maeve's good arm. She had the sexiest forearms, visible with the cuffs of her sweatshirt rolled up. "Are you ready to stand?"

Oh good. More touching. It was like Bianca was trying to torture her.

Maeve nodded and slid her hand against Bianca's, her palm smooth and warm. Bianca was stronger than she looked, and she had Maeve upright before she'd processed the movement, Bianca's other hand coming up to steady Maeve's hip like they were dancing.

Which would have been funny if it didn't cause an uncomfortable flutter in her chest like she was on the verge of a heart attack. She'd really been watching too many cheesy romance movies with Bianca.

"I'm not going to fall," she said when Bianca stood unmoving as she held Maeve in place.

Bianca cleared her throat and shook a look Maeve didn't quite understand out of her eyes before smiling and letting out a light laugh. "Good to know." She stepped away, and Maeve could swear Bianca's fingers trailed along her hip as she let go. "You should drink water. Let me grab you a glass."

She left quickly, and Maeve felt a little bit dazed after what had just happened. Maybe she should have taken up Beth on her offer from this past weekend because her libido was going all kinds of haywire now, after Bianca's light touches had roamed across her body.

Instead of giving in to the idea, she forced herself to sit down on the sofa and put the heating pad back against her shoulder. She let her head rest against the soft cushion and focused her attention on the movie, realizing she'd missed the last twenty minutes.

How would she ever get caught up with the complicated plot now? That sardonic thought almost allowed her to laugh in spite of the nervous energy buzzing through her limbs.

She promised herself that by the time Bianca came back, she'd have herself together. No longing. No wanting. No desperate ache between her legs as she fantasized about pulling Bianca down on top of her when she returned.

Someone like Bianca Rossi deserved the world—or at least far more of it than Maeve could give her.

Chapter Eleven

Bianca wasn't feeling great when Christmas Eve rolled around. She hadn't seen Maeve since Monday. Since Bianca's hands had wandered all over her back in an absolutely not platonic way and Bianca's whole body had lit up like a Roman candle.

And that was a problem for multiple reasons, but the most pressing one was that Maeve was going to arrive at Bianca's parents' house with her dad in less than thirty minutes.

Bianca's brothers, Andrea and Franco, had arrived last night with their wives. Franco's two kids, Luca and Leo, were currently running around the house, chased by Andrea's surprisingly spry four-year-old daughter, Emilia.

It was a madhouse that would usually make her feel all warm and fuzzy inside. Instead, she was anxiously awaiting Maeve's arrival, hoping things were okay between them.

Maeve had seemed okay when she left, if not a little tired. They'd watched the rest of the movie, but Bianca hadn't been paying attention. She'd been sneaking glances at Maeve.

She took a sip of her wine and wandered into the kitchen to see what her dad was doing. Every available surface was covered with various seafood for the Feast of the Seven Fishes they celebrated every year.

God, she hadn't even made sure Maeve ate seafood. Some people were allergic.

She took a deep breath. This would all be fine. It wasn't like Maeve was coming here as her date to meet her family. And even if she didn't like fish, there were two types of pasta, grilled eggplants and zucchini drizzled with olive oil, and a half a dozen loaves of freshly baked bread, courtesy of her mom.

"What's that look?" her dad asked as he lowered another batch of breaded calamari into the deep fryer.

She pulled her festive red sweater tighter around her body. "Maybe it's because it's as cold in here as it is outside. Why are all the windows open?"

"Didn't want to smell up the house." They played this game every year during Feast of the Seven Fishes, where she complained and he ignored her. Lovingly, though. It was their holiday tradition.

"Papa," she said, pulling out all the stops, "I will literally die if it stays this cold." She shivered aggressively to really sell her point.

He waved a pair of tongs at her. "You want the Murphys to come over and have the whole house smelling like a greasy diner?"

"We all work in a bar together. I doubt it will send them running back home." When she met her dad's soft, focused stare, her heart did a little stutter step. "What's wrong?"

"I just want Patrick and Maeve to have a nice night. I know things have been hard for them. The holidays are about family, and this year a huge part of theirs is gone."

She felt unexpected tears welling up behind her eyes, already threatening to spill over. Instead, she stood up a little straighter and took another sip of wine. "I know, Dad. We'll make sure they have a good night."

With her dad's thoughtful words, her perspective and focus shifted so quickly that it almost felt like she'd never been nervous about Maeve's arrival in the first place. He was right. This night was about spending time together and enjoying the holiday. All the other confusion and uncertainty could wait.

* * *

"You can say no to a third helping," Bianca whispered from the seat next to her before shooting Maeve a conspiratorial grin.

The Rossi's had added the spare leaves to their dining room table to make it larger. Right now, nine adults and three children sat comfortably around it. The most surprising thing was that it hadn't bowed under the strain of more food than Maeve had ever seen at one meal. Baked cod, fried calamari, linguine with anchovies, oyster shooters, stuffed lobsters, clams casino, and marinated eel were laid out on the table.

It looked like one of those photos in children's books about old-timey feasts. Not only did everything smell and taste delicious, but it was magnificently plated. When they'd sat down about thirty minutes after arriving, Maeve had wanted to take a few shots with her camera.

It was different from her own holidays growing up, but the overwhelming sentiment of love and family and celebration made her feel warm regardless.

She didn't know what had made her grab her camera before heading out, but since starting to work with Sawyer, she'd started to grow accustomed to having it with her again. She hadn't realized how naked she felt without its weight pressing gently into her side.

And, struck with a sentimentality she didn't often possess,

she thought it could be a nice keepsake for the Rossi's to remember this year.

More than that, having her camera was like wearing an extra layer of protection. She could remove herself a little bit more and think about the night as if she was an observer instead of analyzing how she fit within this group of people. How her mom was conspicuously absent.

So, instead of giving in to the warmth of being part of it, she took a metaphorical, and literal, step back to capture the night.

The kids downed their desserts so fast that Maeve wondered how no one had thrown up on the hardwood floors, but their sugar high presented an excellent opportunity for her to sneak off with them and take some candid shots.

They'd each been able to unwrap a present before dinner, and Bianca had whispered softly in her ear that it had been a tradition she and her brothers had done growing up.

Bianca being close again had felt good. Actual good and scary good and everything in between. Over the week, Maeve had considered more than a few times pretending her strain had flared up just to have a reason for Bianca's hands to be on her again.

Instead, she'd forced herself to meet Sawyer every morning and then go to the bar in the evenings. She still texted Bianca, but not as much as before.

Maeve wondered what it all meant, which was the most annoying part of this whole situation. She never agonized over what women wanted, whether there was a subtle implication in their actions or thoughts or words. For as much as she thought about the world, she took relationships at face value. She was here for a good time, not a long time.

Except now, she found herself thinking about things like what Bianca would look like when she woke up on Christmas morning. Would she come over to her parents' house early to watch the kids open their presents? Would she still make her egg-white omelette with ricotta or eat breakfast here? Would she wear the cute sweater she had on tonight, with the cuffs pushed up so her forearms were visible?

God, Maeve really needed to stop thinking about all the different parts of Bianca's body. Really, she needed to stop thinking about all the parts together too.

Ever since Monday, it was like something inside of her had been knocked loose. She could hear it rattling around no matter what she was doing, like a constant reminder of the effect Bianca had on her.

And Bianca was gorgeous and smart and funny, but she was also so much more than that. She was weird and sweet and thoughtful in the most unexpected ways. That was a long-term problem for the situation given that Maeve generally referred to her disposition on life as being a "Don't Care Bear."

She'd have to let people get close for them to see the messy bits. When she'd been younger and had less confidence, she'd wanted people's approval. Craved it even. For her mother to tell her she'd made it. To keep women wanting more without giving too much of herself. To feel like the work she was doing mattered.

But now? She wanted to see Bianca's nose scrunch in that cute way it did when she was exasperated. To be able to run her hands up Bianca's long legs absently as they watched movies together. And yes, maybe there was that one time when she'd wanted to kiss the little bit of whipped cream from the top of Bianca's lips after an especially aggressive sip of hot cocoa.

What was happening to her?

She didn't have long to dwell on that thought before she was enveloped in the scent of Bianca's light, citrusy perfume and the abstract became reality. She'd know it anywhere. Had spent hours at this point in its proximity.

Bianca's chin came down to rest on her shoulder as they both looked at the Christmas tree, and she instinctively wrapped her fingers tighter around her camera to find some sense of stability. She felt electric, and even though she tried to stop it, her lips twisted into a happy, silly smile she was glad Bianca couldn't see.

All she wanted was to lean back into Bianca's surprisingly solid frame, to have Bianca's arms wrapped around her, their faces brushing and the soft exhales of Bianca's breath tickling her cheek.

But she didn't because that would probably feel more intimate than anything she'd ever done. It had to be this day, trying to deal with the stress of adjusting to her first Christmas without her mom.

"Hey, are you okay?" Bianca asked softly at the same time her hands came down to rest on Maeve's hips.

It was like they were in their own world, separated from the raucous conversation happening in the dining room, the kids having wandered back, likely to beg for permission to open one more gift. Whatever was knocking around inside of her rattled harder, like it was trapped and desperately wanted to break out.

And she didn't... she didn't... she couldn't fight it anymore. Because she knew what the rattling and knocking meant. It was Christmas Eve, and all she wanted was to let go, even for only a few seconds. So she did.

Sighing, she leaned her head back against Bianca's impossibly soft sweater. She shifted her camera into one hand and wrapped her other one around Bianca's wrist, pulling them a little closer together.

Bianca didn't shy away from the touch. Not at all. Instead, she heightened the moment as her hands shifted from Maeve's hips to wrap around her stomach.

Maeve knew she was in a moment that was out of her

control, but she didn't want to stop feeling this way. Because she felt alive. For the first time in months. Maybe for the first time in forever. And it was exciting and terrifying, like her heart was on a roller coaster. She could hear the click in her mind of the car going up and up and up and up, knowing the swoop in her stomach caused by the fall was coming.

"This is really nice," she finally said, still facing the Christmas tree as Bianca held her.

"You looked like you could use a hug. Seems like this is okay?" Bianca's voice was soft, tentative.

"I feel like we keep ending up touching lately."

Bianca lifted her chin from Maeve's shoulder and shifted her head to see her. "I'm a pretty tactile person, but I don't mean to—"

Maeve cut her off. "No. This is good. I didn't realize how much I needed this."

"Well then, you can consider me your personal hug concierge, ready and willing at a moment's notice. I get as much as I give from these, you know." A gentle, teasing tone had found its way into Bianca's voice, and it softened a moment, growing precariously close to becoming what Maeve would have considered romantic, if she'd had any type of experience with romance.

"Is hug cuffing a thing?" Maeve wasn't sure when both of her hands had wrapped around Bianca's wrists, and she'd started idly running her fingers along them in the shape of handcuffs.

She could feel Bianca smile into her shoulder. "You're never going to let me live down bringing that word into your life, are you?"

Maeve usually would have said something sarcastic, but all she could muster up was honesty. "No, probably not."

✦

"It seems like your dad's having a good time. I'm happy about that."

Bianca was right. She'd seen more light in her dad's eyes tonight than in the last six months combined. Sal had kept him busy, with a fresh beer and a funny bowling story any time the conversation was veering into sad territory. He was a little like Bianca in that way, seeming like he always knew the right thing to do in a difficult moment.

"He is," Maeve agreed. "I think this was really good for him. Not easy probably, but still better than us sitting alone at home, together but in separate rooms."

Bianca's steady breathing stilled against Maeve's back. "You wouldn't have celebrated together?"

Maeve allowed herself another indulgent few seconds of enjoying this moment with Bianca before she poked at what still felt like a fresh wound. "My mom loved Christmas. It was her favorite holiday. I always made sure to come home for it, and even though it was just her and my dad, the house was decked out like Santa's Village threw up all over it."

"That sounds like a fun experience. I saw your house a few times over the years after I moved here. Your mom wasn't messing around with her outdoor decorations."

"I think she..." Maeve stalled on her words, trying to figure out the right ones. "I think she wanted to make something that people enjoyed."

She hadn't thought about it a lot. Some people liked to cook. Some people liked to decorate. Some people liked to go to sporting events and cheer on their favorite team. Decorating like a madwoman for Christmas had always just been what her mom had done, for as long as Maeve could remember. But she'd always taken more care with the outdoor decorations, with the lights and inflatable holiday figures and so many candy canes lining the driveway that it was like a solid band of red and white.

Maeve was going to protest when Bianca's hands loosened around her stomach, but the words died on her lips when she was turned gently so they faced one another, her body still wrapped up in Bianca's long arms. Bianca's hair was down, a little mussed from running around with her nephews and niece, and her eyes were a little glassy from the wine she'd had at dinner. She looked so fucking beautiful it felt unreal.

And then she leaned close. Maeve held her breath, wondering if Bianca was going to kiss her, knowing she'd give in to it and wrap her fingers through Bianca's hair at the nape of her neck. She'd probably fist her hand into Bianca's sweater to find purchase, knowing it'd be hard to stand after finally getting to know what Bianca's lips tasted like.

Maeve got her kiss, but not in the way she imagined. Bianca's touch was soft when she placed a light kiss on Maeve's nose, more sweet and comforting than anything. And then she brushed their noses together and smiled at her own gesture before leaning back and looking at Maeve so intently it felt like Bianca could see inside of her.

Cupping her face gently, Bianca ghosted her fingers along Maeve's jaw. "Well, your mom made you, and I enjoy you very much. Merry Christmas, Maeve."

And just like that, the "Don't Care Bear" was starting to care. A lot.

Chapter Twelve

On Monday, Bianca was still coming down from her holiday-induced food coma. Christmas Eve and Christmas Day were followed by a lazy Sunday that was spent indulging in way too many leftovers and watching movies with Jonny.

And thinking. She'd spent a lot of time doing that.

She was still doing all the aforementioned thinking while she organized the waiting room in between patients. Jack had texted her yesterday, asking if she wanted to meet up this week. He hadn't encroached on her holiday time, but he was showing her that he was still interested. She liked that. And she should like him. Well, she should at least like him more.

But, and there was no reason to delude herself any longer, ever since a certain blonde bartender had wandered into her life, it was hard to strike up enthusiasm. Because now she knew how Maeve felt in her arms.

Jonny had teased her again yesterday about whether her boyfriend and girlfriend knew about one another, and honestly, it was starting to feel a little bit like that. Even though nothing sexual was going on with Maeve, Bianca felt like they had a connection.

Did Maeve feel it too? Did she lie in bed like a lovesick teenager, staring at her ceiling and wondering what Bianca was doing the same way Bianca wondered about her? Did she maybe keep her phone a little closer instead of leaving it laying around the house, just so she didn't miss a text?

Bianca really needed to get it together. Her quest for something more serious was putting a damper on her sex life, and even though she knew it wasn't just the proximity to Maeve and her body that was causing Bianca to feel this way, their um... closeness, for lack of a better word, wasn't really helping matters.

How could someone with all those hard edges be so soft?

When she let out a little sound of frustration, she heard Kelly laugh behind her.

"If you organize those newspapers any more forcefully, you're probably going to rub the words off."

Bianca looked down at her hands, where she had a stack of newspaper perfectly aligned, her fingers crumpling the edges. She smiled sheepishly and placed them on the end table before turning toward Kelly. "Got a little distracted."

Kelly studied her for a second before she seemed to accept the answer. "Did you have a good holiday?"

Just held Maeve in my arms as we looked at the Christmas tree before I did this weird thing where I gave her a nose kiss and practically word-vomited my feelings all over her. "Sure. It was great. How was yours?"

"Busy. Luna insisted on wearing her Batman costume to Christmas dinner. Quinn, who's apparently been trying to cultivate her cooking skills, brought more side dishes than could fit in my kitchen. The turkey spent an hour in the oven before I realized it wasn't on." Kelly pointed at herself. "I take responsibility for that one."

Bianca laughed. "Sounds like a family gathering of the truest form."

"It was," Kelly said with a sincere smile. "Was it just you and your parents, or did your brothers and their families come up?"

She loved that Kelly always remembered the little details. It was probably going to make it impossible for Luna and Ella to get away with things as they got older, but in a friend, it was a fantastic quality.

"There were twelve of us. My immediate family, and then the Murphys came too."

"I'm glad you were all together. Mrs. Murphy always loved Christmas. I'm sure she'd be happy to know that Patrick and Maeve were surrounded by love."

"Yeah, it was... nice," was the word Bianca settled on, though it didn't come close to scratching the full scope of emotions she'd felt.

And she'd liked feeling them. The anticipation and hopefulness and excitement that came from being around Maeve. She wanted to lean into that despite knowing it wasn't a great idea.

Her attention was pulled when the chime above the door signaled that the ten a.m. appointment had arrived. She gave Kelly a playful eye roll and headed back to her desk.

Once she had the arrival checked in, she grabbed her phone out of the drawer she'd hidden it in to stop looking every few minutes to see if Maeve had texted.

Even if she wasn't ready to admit to herself that she was chasing Maeve, she could at least admit she was chasing the feeling she felt whenever they were together.

Cuffing Season

* * *

Maeve was watching Shirley complete her last set on the shoulder press when her phone vibrated in her hand.

Bianca Rossi – 9:53 a.m.
Movie night tonight? :)

She smiled reflexively as her stomach fluttered. She hadn't talked to Bianca since Christmas Eve, with the exception of a quick Merry Christmas text the following day that hadn't led to more conversation.
Bianca, she knew, was busy with her boisterous family, so she'd kept her distance.

Maeve Murphy – 9:54 a.m.
Are they still Christmas movies since the holiday's over?

Bianca Rossi – 9:54 a.m.
I like to think of Christmas as a state of mind. As long as my decorations are up, Christmas movie watching will happen.

Maeve Murphy – 9:54 a.m.
I assume it still looks like The North Pole in your house?

Bianca Rossi – 9:54 a.m.

You know it! You should bring some of your photography tonight. I'd love to take a look at it.

Shirley's indigent huff pulled her focus from responding to Bianca's message.

"Yes, Shirley?"

"What if I'd dropped the weights and crushed myself?"

"It's a machine. You know it doesn't even work like that."

Shirley shot her an impish grin. "Maybe not, but it's rude to not pay attention to the person you're with to stare at a screen."

Maeve rolled her eyes. Shirley, she'd learned, was seventy-two and retired from a lifelong career as a postal worker. Complete with a full pension and retirement benefits. "Shirley, I appreciate the outlook, but I don't think you understand. I have a job for my dad where I need to make sure I don't need to cover any shifts, and I have a freelance job. Add the other jobs I'm trying to get, ahead of returning to New York City, and it's not really possible for me to float along dreamily like I'm in control of my own day."

Well, maybe that was a little dramatic, and it was clear Shirley thought so too. "Phooey!" She stood up and walked over to the cleaning station. When she returned with a paper towel and spray to wipe down the machine, she looked at Maeve seriously. "People are always going to want your time. They're always going to want your energy. No one feels like there are enough hours in the day, and it's up to you to decide how much to give. Whether giving it is worth it."

God, Maeve couldn't remember the last time she'd had anyone try to give her life advice. "I know."

Shirley waved her off. "I know your generation is getting stuck with a raw deal. Pensions don't exist. Forget about staying at a company forever even if you wanted to. I get it. I really do.

But there's always going to be something shitty that's holding you back from feeling like you 'have it all.' My mother was a housewife with six kids. She absolutely hated it, but that's just what you did back then. Two of my brothers got shipped off to Vietnam, and one didn't come back. Life is not fair, and it's never been fair, sometimes more so to some groups than others. All I know is that if you answer your phone every time you get a message, you're setting the tone that you're always available."

Maeve was strangely transfixed by what Shirley was telling her, surprised at how much sense it was making. Because she was a little lost, a little unsure of what to do next. Her initial comment had been to get Shirley to leave her alone about it, since she'd been texting with Bianca and wanted to be available for that. But Shirley was making some damn good points about the rest of it. "So... how do I manage it?"

"You've gotta find your north stars. Maybe that's a career or something you're passionate about or love or having a family. Pick your non-negotiables and then build around those. Don't get caught up in the race to the bottom. It hurts you, and ultimately, it hurts everyone else except those that want something from you and can get it cheaper and faster than your body or mind can handle."

Maeve nodded. Now she was hanging on every word. She did feel like she was always chasing and clamoring and struggling just to stay above water. No matter how hard she tried to fit all the pieces together, nothing ever felt quite comfortable.

"What are yours?"

Shirley considered the question before answering. "Fitness is one. I had a health scare about ten years ago that made me realize if I didn't get it together, I probably wasn't making it to seventy. I have a group of friends I see twice a week. I make sure to visit my partner's grave once a week. She died five years ago."

The emotion hit Maeve quickly, like a punch in the gut. Grief was a powerful thing, and she didn't know if she'd ever be able to talk so casually about her mom's death without making it into some darkly twisted joke. That was easier than finding words for the emptiness that expanded and contracted in her body at the most random times, that sometimes happened so quickly it felt like she couldn't breathe.

"That's..." She let out a steadying breath, realizing she was on the verge of crying. "That's a good list."

"It's the list for now, and it makes me happy. Maybe it will change. Maybe it won't. Life has a funny way of taking us in strange directions." It seemed like Shirley had used up her supply of prophetic wisdom for the day, and she took a long sip from her water bottle and then shrugged her shoulders like that was that.

"Okay. Um... I have to go meet Sawyer for my morning job, but..."

"Yes, I'll be here Wednesday and Friday. Normal time."

Maeve nodded. She wasn't good at this whole talking about feelings thing. And honestly, she wasn't sure she wanted to get better at it given how clammy her hands were just then.

Shirley threw her towel over her shoulder. "I'll see you Wednesday," she said, taking a few steps away from Maeve before she turned around. "And I know that wasn't a work text. You were smiling too much. Looks like maybe you're already on track to find one of your north stars."

* * *

Bianca was on her way to the grocery store after work, ahead of Maeve's arrival. She hit number three on her favorites before she could second-guess herself. She needed some advice, even if it was probably a horrible idea.

Jonny's voice floated through her speakers. "Hey, babe. I'm just wrapping up at the office. I'm surprised you didn't text."

"I'm driving. And I didn't want there to be a paper trail in case you tried to use it against me later."

"Oh, this sounds good. Let me sit down so I can prepare myself."

She could hear Jonny sitting back down in his leather office chair. "Did you just put your feet up?"

"I do my best work horizontally, thinking included."

Bianca rolled her eyes. "I'm going to ignore that part."

Seconds of silence passed between them until she heard Jonny's voice again. "Are you going to tell me what this is about, or am I supposed to guess?"

Well, Bianca guessed she was really doing this. She cleared her throat. "How do you know if someone likes you?"

Jonny's laugh boomed so loudly through the car she could feel her steering wheel vibrate. "Bianca. Everyone likes you. It's only a matter of whether or not you like them."

"That's not helpful, Jonny. And also, it's not true."

"Fine. Is this about your boyfriend or your girlfriend?"

"I wish you'd stop calling them both that."

"Because you don't like it or because it's not true?"

"I'm barely dating Jack and I'm not dating Maeve at all, so let's say a little bit of column A, a little bit of column B."

"Okay, so which one is it about?"

Bianca rolled into the grocery store parking lot and dropped her head against the steering wheel. "Maeve."

She could practically feel the energy radiating from Jonny through the speakers. "Perfect. I knew it. I knew you liked her."

"I didn't say I liked her. I asked how I know if someone likes me. Please, Jonny. This is serious," she said, exasperation seeping into her voice.

"First of all, you're a catch, B. Don't forget that. Secondly, why are you asking me this?"

"I just..." Bianca lifted her head back into an upright position and chewed at her lip. "Sometimes I feel like we have these moments. And I wonder if she's feeling them too. That's all."

"Please explain." The teasing from his voice was gone, replaced with an earnest interest in whatever Bianca was about to say.

Bianca hadn't felt this out of her depth since she'd realized she had a crush on Rachel Keaton in the seventh grade.

"I don't really know how to describe it. Like... she's receptive to whatever I say, but she doesn't really push anything herself. You know?"

"Are you confused because someone that could be sexually attracted to you can sit in a room with you and not try to rip your clothes off?"

Bianca huffed. "No. And it's not just about that. I mean, sure, she's really attractive, but we've grown closer, and I don't know, I kinda feel like there's something there. I just don't know if she's feeling it too."

"Well, let's say she is feeling it. What would you do about it?"

Bianca didn't want to admit to Jonny how far her mind had been wandering lately, especially since their massage last week. "I don't know. She's probably only going to be here for a few more weeks."

"So you want to sleep with her to see if it would be as good as you think it would be, but you're conflicted because you don't just want casual hookups." Could he read her mind? She really needed to stop spending so much time with him.

"Okay, that was actually pretty spot-on."

"I say go for it."

Cuffing Season

Bianca's hands tightened around the steering wheel. "Could you please repeat that?"

"Look, I haven't seen you agonizing over someone like this since you've lived here. You're always being chased. Chasing looks good on you, girl. I say you go get your woman."

"What if I'm misreading the signals?"

"Meh. Worst-case scenario is she's leaving soon anyway and you shot your shot."

"You say it like it's just easy to be rejected."

Jonny laughed breezily. She could imagine him primping his hair in the mirror she knew that he kept in his desk drawer. "It gets easier with practice. I think if you know what you want, you owe it to yourself to go for it."

"She's got a lot going on right now. I don't want to add to it."

"If she's into it, it won't be an imposition. Trust me."

Looking down at the clock on her dashboard, she realized how much time had passed. "Okay, thanks for the pep talk. I'll think about it."

"You realize I expect a full report on how things go, right?"

"If it goes well, sure. If it doesn't, then we never had this conversation."

"What conversation?"

She smiled and grabbed her bag off the passenger's seat. "That's why I love you. Okay, gotta run into the store. Talk later?"

"You better believe it."

Chapter Thirteen

Maeve hated being late. She knew it went against the whole disaffected thing she had going, but she was chronically early if she could help it.

Tonight wasn't shaping up to be one of those nights.

She'd started working on a series of photos from some of the larger items that had just arrived at the Victorian house from the old antiques shop downtown, and the day had gotten away from her.

By the time she realized how late it had gotten, she'd had just enough time to rush home and shower for the second time that day. Photography could be a surprisingly physical endeavor with the angles she needed to get into for the best shot.

And after her conversation with Shirley earlier, she'd decided to put her phone on mute while working with Sawyer. Maybe she hadn't quite figured out any of her north stars, or whatever Shirley called them, but she knew that it was hard keeping up with all of her commitments, which was compounded when she tried to stay on top of texts and emails in between it all.

So for the six hours she'd been with Sawyer, she'd kept her phone in her bag. She was pretty proud she hadn't checked it once, and it was actually kind of nice to fully focus on what she was doing while she was doing it.

Except, as she'd rushed home to shower, she'd remembered leaving Bianca's text unanswered earlier in the day.

After showering and drying her hair, she responded to Bianca.

Maeve Murphy – 5:45 p.m.
Will bring if I can find them. They're in a box somewhere.

When she'd found out her mom had died in the car accident, it had felt like time had stopped. She didn't know why at the time, but she knew she had to come home indefinitely. Her mom had already passed away when she'd gotten the news, so there was no immediate jumping on a train to get back to Kingsford.

Her mom had died on a Monday. Until very recently, she hadn't cared for them very much because of that. That seemed fair.

Everything in the common spaces of her old apartment belonged to roommates who'd been there longer than her, so, without really processing it, she'd packed up her stuff into boxes and had been lucky enough to get a small U-Haul the next day.

Besides two suitcases stuffed with clothing, she hadn't unpacked any of the dozen or so boxes that made up the entirety of her life in New York, but then again, people didn't live in New York to collect things. They collected experiences. Maeve had a lot of those, but thinking back, it was hard to remember who she'd been with or how she'd felt. That bothered her, but she didn't have time to dwell on it right then.

The dozen boxes were stacked in their freezing garage. The main light had gone out and her dad hadn't replaced it, so she fumbled over, leaving the door connecting the garage and house open to provide a hint of illumination.

By the time she'd opened two of the boxes, her fingers were numb from the cold. On the third box, one of the smaller ones, she saw one of her albums that had at least some of her pieces printed. It would do.

She closed the flaps on the box and headed back through the house. In five minutes, she was on her way to Bianca's, pulling up with a minute to spare.

"Fuck yeah," she muttered to herself as she prepared for the quick run from the car to the house.

The front door opened as she was making her way up the steps onto Bianca's porch, which was also, and unsurprisingly, still festively decorated for the season.

And then Bianca was standing in front of her, the light from inside haloing her as she leaned on the doorframe in an oversized sweater and leggings. For a second, Maeve was struck by the realization that coming home to this sight every night wouldn't be a hardship at all, even in a town like Kingsford.

She dodged right around that thought like she was a professional freeze tag player and hopped up the steps, seeking the warmth just as much as she was running from her own racing mind.

"You found them," Bianca said with a bright smile as she stepped to the side to let Maeve pass. She had no intention of slowing down at the promise of heat.

Cuffing Season

Maeve walked the box over to the coffee table and put it down. "Don't get your hopes up. I'm not sure what I brought, so it could be from my phase where I liked to take out-of-focus shots of pigeons in Central Park."

Bianca's eyes tracked across Maeve's face before her lips curled into a smile. "I can never tell if you're being serious or not."

With a shrug, Maeve moved toward the kitchen. "See for yourself. Can I get a glass of water? I've basically been a photography machine today, and I forgot to drink water."

"Obviously yes to the water. But... wouldn't that make you a camera?"

Maeve laughed and grabbed a glass. "If we're getting technical, sure."

Bianca sat down on the sofa in front of the box, and Maeve downed half the glass in a single gulp.

This was good. Things felt relatively normal between them. Maeve wasn't acting like some sort of lovesick teenager, and Bianca hadn't made mention of their embrace from Christmas Eve.

She was filling up her glass again when Bianca let out an, "Oh," from where she sat on the sofa. One of her legs was tucked under her, with her body leaning over the box to peer inside. And dangling from her fingers was...

If there was a god, he must think fucking with Maeve was a pretty good time. Because honestly, she had barely been functional while she'd packed. Sheets had gone in boxes with notebooks. Lotions had gone in boxes with backpacks. And apparently, some of her photos has gone in boxes with her collection of sex toys.

Which meant that between Bianca's long, slender fingers dangled a pair of black restraint cuffs.

"Is this because I told you about cuffing season?" Bianca

asked, her voice a little higher than normal. And her cheeks were tinged an amazing shade of pink that made her look flushed, and yeah... that was really working for Maeve just then, even if she didn't know that she could string a coherent sentence together.

Maeve thought for agonizing seconds about taking the out Bianca had given her. It would be easy to explain it away as a joke.

"I packed in a hurry leaving New York. I guess I didn't really remember what I put where."

Bianca sat up a little straighter. "Do you mind if I look at them?"

Maeve wasn't sure what was happening, but the tenuous sense of normalcy she'd felt moments ago had evaporated. She wasn't sure what to do with Bianca's curiosity except be incredibly turned on by it.

She took a quick, steadying breath. "Those were a gift, so um... they've never actually been used. I just didn't want you to think that, like... well, I'm not sure what you're thinking right now, but..." Maeve tried to roll her shoulder subtly to ease some of the tension and let out another exhale. "What I mean is, sure. You can absolutely look at them."

Was Maeve trying to make herself suffer? Watching Bianca pull the cuffs apart until the chain connecting them went taut made heat sprawl wildly across her body, radiating down to her center.

But friends talked about sex. This didn't need to be weird. Maeve was making it weird, she realized, by standing across the room and watching Bianca like a voyeur.

After she grabbed her refilled glass of water, she walked slowly over to the sofa and sat at the opposite end. And then there really was nothing to do but watch Bianca study the cuffs, her fingers rubbing against the soft faux fur lining the inside of the bands.

They'd been a gift from a girl she was hooking up with, except things had fizzled before they'd ever gotten the chance to use them. It was a strange irony that here she was, with Bianca of all people, seeing them in the hands of someone else for the first time.

Bianca let them fall again, and Maeve was hypnotized by the rhythmic swaying. It would have all been fine. Maeve would have been able to push past this if Bianca hadn't said her next words.

"I prefer the satin ones, but these are nice too."

* * *

Had Bianca pushed things too far? She thought maybe she had, given how Maeve had become extremely interested in putting on a movie as soon as she'd brought up satin restraints.

They were both adults. She'd seen Maeve's box of surprises, and all she was trying to do was convey that it was a completely normal thing.

Okay, well... she knew that wasn't exactly true. She'd been testing the waters, but it was pretty clear that hadn't worked out like she'd hoped. But she wasn't even sure what she'd hoped would happen. That Maeve's eyes would light up and they'd drag one another back to the bedroom, shedding clothing as they went?

It wasn't like Bianca hadn't thought about it more than a few times over the last hour as they'd been watching the movie. Why didn't these movies ever have sex? It was all she could think about right then.

And Maeve looked so cute on her side, cuddled up with her

feet on the sofa, legs bent at the knees. She was leaning on the arm of the sofa, her face resting in her palm.

Bianca had been warring with herself over pangs of want and then flutters of butterflies.

What she needed to do was focus on the movie, but all she wanted to do was coax Maeve closer so they could cuddle.

"Oh, come on!" Maeve's voice was like a gunshot that cut through Bianca's inner ramblings.

Except that she had no idea what was going on in said movie. She'd been too distracted. "Something not to your liking? Did you spot a boom mic in the frame?"

Maeve turned, the cutest, most frustrated scowl on her face. "They both need to get their heads out of their asses. Of course he likes her. And it's obvious she likes him. Why are they circling one another like idiots?"

That was not what Bianca had been expecting, though at least she'd already seen this one and knew enough to vaguely keep up. "I mean, cheesy as these movies are, there's something to be said for it looking easier to see when you're on the outside of it."

Bianca realized she had a golden opportunity, and she didn't want to waste it. She paused the movie and looked at Maeve intently.

* * *

"Haven't you ever been in a situation where you're not sure what page the other person's on?"

Not until I met you, were the words that threatened to tumble out, but Maeve held them in like her life depended on it. "I don't know that I've ever been in a situation that's serious enough for that."

Bianca lifted a brow. "Meaning?"

"I just don't think it's something I ever prioritized before. What you said a few weeks ago about people in New York City is true, at least in my experience. There are so many things going on that it felt like people met when it made sense and drifted when it made sense. There wasn't a lot of intention to grow together or whatever." Poetic, Maeve. As usual.

Bianca looked at the paused television, and Maeve missed the warmth of her stare immediately. "That's fair."

"What about you?" Maeve asked, wanting more than anything for Bianca to look at her again, to feel the exact thing she was denying to Bianca.

"What about me?" Bianca bit her bottom lip, and it was an unfairly attractive visual that Maeve did not need to see just then.

"Have you ever been seeing someone or liked someone but you weren't sure how they felt?"

Bianca eased both her long legs underneath herself and tilted her head to the side. "Guys are usually pretty easy. Maybe you don't know if they really like you as something serious, but they are fairly overt if they're interested."

"I kinda figured you'd intimidate guys."

"Why's that?"

Maeve had walked right into that one. "Because you're exceptionally attractive."

Bianca gave her a self-deprecating smile. "I was around a lot of other pretty people too." She watched as Bianca laid her arm down on the back of the sofa and leaned her head against her hand. "But what I was going to say earlier is that while guys are usually easy, it's the women that were way more confusing."

When Maeve had thought she'd get better at girl talk by hanging out with Bianca, this wasn't what she'd had in mind. "Oh... You haven't mentioned that before."

"I haven't dated any women seriously since moving back

home. I thought I was in love with another model, Nia, but we weren't on the same page." Bianca's shoulders dropped slightly, and she pulled her focus to look around the room before her eyes drew back to Maeve, a renewed purpose in them. "Actually, that's not true. I was in love with her. She wasn't in love with me."

"That must have been disappointing," was all that Maeve could come up with. Her mind was going in a million different directions, and all of them started and ended with the fact that Bianca dated women.

"It was," Bianca finally answered.

"So she, like... broke your heart?" Maeve really needed to learn to be a better conversationalist.

"She made me realize that I didn't just want to keep having flings. It hurt to be rejected, sure. It especially hurt to not realize we were on the same page, but ultimately, falling in love with her made me realize that's what I wanted. To love someone and know they're mine and I'm theirs. I have a pretty good sense of myself, and now I want to know what it feels like to be an us."

Maeve couldn't imagine a world where anyone that wasn't certifiably insane would walk away from Bianca. And even if it was physically difficult to push her words out, she did it anyway. "Well, I have no doubt you'll find that person."

It almost felt like too much, the way Bianca looked at her then, how her eyes tracked across Maeve's features before dropping down to her lips, like she was waiting for Maeve to say something more. When she was met with Maeve's silence, she pulled her stare back up, the green in her eyes so bright Maeve felt like she was staring into emeralds. And for a moment, she thought she could see want in Bianca's eyes, but maybe it was just a reflection from her own.

"I'm sure you're right," Bianca said quietly before she

cleared her throat and reached toward the coffee table for the remote.

Later, when Maeve was driving home, the realization hit her so hard she almost pulled off the road. Shirley's words from earlier in the day that she'd put away in a deep recess of her mind, the same way she'd put away her phone to get space to focus, slammed into her consciousness with a force she couldn't ignore.

Bianca's eyes hadn't looked like emeralds—they'd looked like stars.

Chapter Fourteen

Bianca swirled her straw around in her drink. "I don't know why we needed to come here, Jonny. It's not like I ask to go to your place of work and spend time there."

"I'm an accountant, love. And while I do keep a bottle of gin in my desk when things are truly desperate, it's not exactly the type of place to let loose for the evening."

Jonny had insisted they come to Murph's for their Wednesday night hangout. No doubt because she'd been insufferably—his word—tight-lipped about her night with Maeve on Monday.

"I'm not going to get shit-faced where I work regardless, so you picked a doubly bad place to come. And I know what you're doing."

He glanced toward Maeve at the other end of the bar before swiveling in his chair to level a charming smile in her direction. "And what's that?"

Bianca glared at him. "I'm not dignifying that with a response."

"Maybe I want to see how things have been progressing. So sue me," he said with an unapologetic shrug.

She lowered her voice and leaned toward him. "Do not embarrass me. She's a coworker."

He tipped his drink toward her. "And unrequited crush."

"I swear to god, Jonny... if you say anything...."

"You'll what? Stop being my friend when your crush leaves and be two friends down?"

"That wasn't a nice thing to say," she pouted.

"I know. I'm sorry." She appreciated that he seemed genuinely sincere, even if he was usually apologizing for putting his foot in his mouth. He turned his attention back toward Maeve. "She is cute. If you're into that whole small, angry thing... which apparently you are," he finished as he turned to face her again.

"She's not angry. Usually."

"I'm curious, though. What do you like about her? I mean, at least it will be helpful for future prospects since she's got you spinning."

Bianca smiled in spite of how royally fucked she was right then. She couldn't even pretend to muster up some kind of flippant answer. The words were already on the tip of her tongue since she'd spent almost every free minute since Monday thinking about Maeve. "I like that she didn't blink twice about coming home and helping her dad, even though they have a strained relationship. And I like that she does things without making a big deal out of them. She doesn't need the praise that most people want when they do the right thing. And I like how she has this little dimple in her cheek that only comes out when she's really smiling." She gave him a pointed look. "You probably haven't seen it. She doesn't like you very much."

"Oh, wow. So you *like her*, like her. Not just in an 'I want to rip your clothing off' kind of way." Jonny looked so aghast, like she'd just told him Santa Claus wasn't real.

She snuck a glance down the bar at Maeve, who was pouring a beer. Maeve caught her eye and smiled before pushing the drink across the bar to the customer. Bianca thought she could almost see the dimple in her cheek from here. "I mean, I want to rip her clothing off too."

"So, how's this going to play out? You're just going to be star-crossed lovers until she leaves?"

Bianca sighed and tried to hide the disappointment in her voice. "Look at how I'm acting. If we actually hooked up, imagine how much worse it would be when she leaves."

"At least I'd get to eat ice cream with you all the time and pretend it's because I'm being a good friend."

"So noble of you, bestie," she said, patting his hand.

"How'd you guys leave things on Monday night? Did you make your intentions clear for her hand in marriage?"

She snort-laughed and gave him a light push. "I hate you so much."

"I just think you're overthinking this. Putting the cart before the horse and all that." He waved his hand flippantly, like he always did when he was actually giving good advice but wanted to pretend he didn't care. "I asked around about her, you know," he added casually.

Bianca used her body to distract Jonny from an attractive man walking by that she knew would pull his attention. "Excuse me? What do you mean by that?"

"I asked my sister, Amelia, if she remembered her. She's three years older than me, so they would have been in the same grade. I thought that was pretty smart of me."

It had surprised Bianca that there wasn't anyone from high school Maeve wanted to connect with after returning home.

With Jonny practically vibrating in his seat, her curiosity got the better of her. "And?"

"Well, Amelia dug out an old yearbook, and let's just say that's thirty minutes of my life I'll never get back."

"Jonny..."

"Fine. So she only vaguely remembered her? Which is weird because it's not a huge school. Mostly, she said she was quiet, thought of by the other kids as kinda weird. Did her own thing, but she always had a camera with her."

Bianca snuck another glance down the bar. "That sounds like Maeve."

"She hasn't come over to say hi yet. Did you do something on Monday that I should know about?"

Maeve was busy, sure, but it had seemed a little weird that Pete, the bartender who worked the other nights, had been the one helping them. Though to be fair, Bianca had sat on his side of the bar since Jonny was with her, and she could never quite guarantee what would or wouldn't come out of his mouth in a public setting. She knew Maeve was going to be a topic of conversation.

"No."

He leaned in close and matched the tone of her voice. "Then why are we whispering?"

"We're not."

"I feel like I need to shove my ear in your mouth to hear you right now."

Bianca scrunched up her face when the visual formed in her brain. "Ugh, Jonny. No."

"You have to talk to her before we leave. I deserve this."

"You deserve this?" Bianca asked incredulously. "My abysmal love life is not free entertainment for you."

"Think of it as my Christmas gift."

She stared him down. "Your Christmas gift was me agreeing to come here in the first place."

"Oh! Oh! She's coming over here. Look natural." He splayed his hands across the bar and leaned down on his forearm in quite possibly the most unnatural pose Bianca had ever seen.

"Jonny," she warned quietly as Maeve closed the last few feet of space between them and stood on the other side of the bar. "Hey, Maeve. How's it going?"

* * *

Maeve had to go say hello. She knew that. Except that she'd already spent the last forty-eight hours doing little else but think about Bianca, and seeing her at the other end of the bar had thrown her for a little bit of a loop.

So instead of going over right away and making a fool of herself, especially with Jonny in tow, she'd waited. And then, after an agonizing thirty minutes, she'd realized that if she made this about work, she might be able to get through it without saying something stupid.

But Bianca looked so pretty, in a soft, deep V-neck sweater that highlighted the green in her eyes. Her hair was completely down, falling in light waves and framing her expressive features.

Maeve knew it would feel amazing to run her fingers through Bianca's hair, and she knew it would feel even better to taste the shiny gloss on her lips.

"Get it together," she whispered to herself at the same time Bianca said hi. Her eyes went wide, hoping Bianca hadn't heard her. Either way, she'd pretend she hadn't. "Hey, guys. Decided to check out Kingsford's premiere Wednesday night food and beverage establishment?"

Bianca gave her a slightly strange look, but it was Jonny who spoke next. "Maeve, lovely to see you as always."

She nodded toward him. "Jonny," she said before turning back to Bianca. "I know I'm the absolute worst, but can I talk to you about work for approximately three minutes? No more, I promise. I just wanted to check in about Friday."

"Sure. What's up?"

"I'm not sure if you were planning on working Friday, so I wanted to confirm. Pete's going to be on anyway since it's New Year's Eve. So... well..." God, it was always harder than normal to find the words that were already difficult to find when she was around Bianca. "Anyway, the point is, if you have plans, or want to make plans, we can cover without you."

"Oh," Bianca said, a little crease forming between her brows. "I was planning on working."

"I mean... I didn't know if you and Jack..." It seemed like a safe way to bring up a question she'd wanted to ask, even if Jonny's presence for the conversation wasn't ideal.

"I don't have plans with Jack."

"He asked. She declined," Jonny chimed in.

"Jonny." Bianca's voice was sharp, exasperation evident across her features.

"What? I'm just telling the truth."

"The point is," Bianca said as she turned her attention back to Maeve, "I'm planning on being here on Friday night if that works for you."

"Sure. The help would be appreciated."

"Then I'll see you on New Year's Eve." Bianca arched her brow, and Maeve wondered if there was an implication in her words.

True to her word, for her own sanity as much as respecting Bianca's time, Maeve was gone from their side of the bar within three minutes of arriving. And even in an amount of time as insignificant as that, it felt like she was a little punchdrunk from their conversation. Then again, she always felt like that when she was around Bianca.

She was torn when Bianca and Jonny left after one more drink, dutifully served by Pete. The rest of her shift loomed, looking a lot less inviting without Bianca to sneak glances at from across the bar.

When had she so totally and completely lost her edge?

And, more than that, why didn't she care?

* * *

When Bianca dropped Jonny off at his house, he gave her a pointed look, which tipped her off that some sort of tough love was coming.

"Just say it, Jonny."

"I saw the way she looked at you."

"And what way might that be?"

"Like she wants to fuck you senseless and then cuddle up with you to take a nap. Ya know, just what dreams are truly made of."

"We were talking about work." His mind was truly a place of amazement.

"She asked about Jack, which implies interest on her part to know if you're still seeing him."

Bianca rolled her eyes. "And wasn't it just so helpful of you to share that I'd declined his invitation."

"What can I say? I'm a good friend."

"You're an absolute pain is what you are."

"Look," Jonny said, getting serious in a way he often didn't, "I know it seems messy and complicated and whatever else, but I think you'll regret not taking this chance. Life's too short to have regrets like that."

"It's not about having regrets; it's about sticking to my boundaries. She said she's going back to New York. She said she doesn't really do serious relationships."

"In the abstract, but you haven't plucked up the courage to tell her you like her. The wondering is the worst part. I think you should just take a chance." Jonny opened his car door, and she shivered from the incoming cold. He ducked his head back down. "Just think about it. Don't be a chicken."

"Did you really just call me a chicken?"

He shut her car door and ran toward his house, flailing his arms out at his sides and yelling, "*Bock bock*," loud enough that she could hear it.

God, she loved that man, even if she hated him a little bit right then too.

* * *

On Friday morning, Maeve was making coffee in the kitchen after her workout when her dad walked in. That wasn't surprising, but she did stop in her tracks when he sat down at the kitchen table with his own cup of coffee.

"Heading into the bar soon?" she asked. Was she supposed to sit down at the table too? Was it rude to go back to her room like she usually did?

"I was hoping we could talk for a few minutes."

Maeve stopped short, her coffee cup a few inches from her mouth. She lowered it back onto the counter, hoping whatever came next wasn't horrible. Why else would he want to talk except to tell her he was dying or she was dying or... Why he would know she was dying before she did wasn't relevant. "What's up?"

She realized as she stared at him that she hadn't really looked at him in a while, probably in months. They'd been inhabiting the same spaces but were so far removed from one another's existences they might as well be strangers.

But as she looked into his eyes, a similar shade of blue to her own, he looked... happier? At least like a little bit of the light was starting to come back into them.

He leaned his forearm on the kitchen table that Maeve felt like they'd had since she was born, which they probably had, and tightened his hand around his coffee cup. "I know you were planning on leaving soon, and well..." He cleared his throat. "I wanted to thank you."

Whatever Maeve had prepared herself to hear, it wasn't that. She picked up her cup again before placing it back on the counter. God, she was bad at this. Maybe as bad as her father, but at least he'd plucked up the will to have a conversation with her.

She cleared her throat, realizing it was exactly the same way he'd done it moments ago. "I appreciate you saying that. Despite our differences, I wouldn't have done anything else. It's what Mom would have wanted."

"Differences?" The slightly confused stare he gave her almost broke Maeve's heart.

Did he really not see how at odds they'd been for most of Maeve's adolescent and adult life? Definitely since she'd decided she wanted to leave Kingsford and do something else with her life besides languish in some little riverside town.

Guess they were doing this. She picked up her mug for the third time in less than a minute and walked over to the table. She picked the seat across from him, like they were both sitting down for an important meeting. It was a conversation that was long overdue anyway, whether her mom was around or not.

She eased into her chair and thought about all the family dinners they'd shared when she was growing up. Since she'd been back, she couldn't remember a single time she and her dad had sat here together. She was acutely aware of the fact that weeks ago, she probably couldn't have had this conversation. And it was painfully obvious who'd helped her get to this point. But she'd worry about that later. "Our differences, as in you never really supporting me leaving."

As she searched his face, she was struck by how sincerely confused he was, and his next words caused a dull ache in her chest. "If I've ever made you feel like I didn't support you or your life, I'm sorry for that. I just wanted you to have at least one voice in your life that wasn't making you feel like you needed to leave to find happiness."

"But..." She was struggling to find the right words. They were doing so well, but there was a delicate undercurrent that made her feel like she could be swept away at any moment. "I didn't want what I wanted because Mom said I should." Though, as she said the words out loud, she didn't know if they were true or not. She'd been lost and awkward as a kid, and the idea her mother had given her, that there was a bigger life out there waiting for her, had been an immense comfort.

It was like her dad could read her mind. Maybe they weren't as different as she thought. "Your mom wanted you to have a big life. She wanted you to have big adventures and big dreams. She wanted you to do all the things maybe she never really felt like she got to do. I always thought maybe she felt a little bit like the grass was always greener. I love you both so much, and I just want you to be happy with whatever life you're leading."

Her stomach was heavy, but most surprising were the tears that were pooling behind her eyes. She wasn't used to anything coming close to this level of emotion, except if it was something she understood like lust or anger or frustration.

How could she have so misconstrued his intentions? "So

you haven't disapproved this whole time of the way I've been living my life?"

"God, no," he said with a boisterous laugh that cut the intensity of the moment. "I don't care what you do with your life, Maeve. All I want is for you to be happy. If living in New York City is what makes you happy, then I'll support you however I can. I can't begin to express how much your help has meant to me these last months. Whatever you do, you're an amazing woman, and I'm so proud of you."

Maeve didn't want to be crying at ten a.m. in her kitchen, but here she was, the tears pricking behind her eyes finally spilling over and down her cheeks. "I love you, Dad."

As her dad's "I love you, too," reverberated between them, she couldn't help but think about all the other things she'd been wrong about.

Chapter Fifteen

Bianca pushed a drink across the bar to Kelly, who was ordering for herself, Sawyer, and Quinn. The happy couple was over at a small table, making gooey eyes at one another. "There's no way you're making it until midnight."

"Oh, don't I know it," Kelly said as she held up her highball glass. "I'm giving myself a nine p.m. cutoff time to get home to Trevor and the girls."

After looking at her wrist, to a watch she wasn't wearing, Bianca met Kelly's happy smile. "Looks like you have about two hours to go crazy then."

"What's this place going to look like in a few hours?"

Bianca honestly didn't know. "I've never worked here on New Year's Eve. My dad's doing a limited food menu that ends at ten, and besides a champagne toast at midnight, I assume it will be business as usual."

Kelly looked around the growing crowd before glancing at Maeve, who was on her side of the bar, pouring drinks like a madwoman. "How's Maeve doing?"

Again, Bianca honestly didn't know. She'd been surprised

when she'd arrived that night to see Maeve and her dad at the end of the bar together, heads drawn close while they chatted about something. Maeve had given her a broad smile, complete with the dimple Bianca loved to see.

But quickly the crowd had grown, and they hadn't had a chance to talk before they were relegated to their separate ends of the bar. Throw in Pete in the section between them, and she'd only caught a few glimpses of Maeve in the last hour.

"She seems good. Why so curious about Maeve?"

Kelly shrugged and picked up all three drinks with impressive dexterity. "Sawyer seems to like working with her. Guess I'm just trying to see what all the fuss is about," Kelly said with a playful wink before she turned and headed back to her table.

Get in line, Bianca thought as she pulled her attention back to the bar. Sitting in front of her was Jack, a sweet smile on his face.

"I'm here with work friends," he said, holding up his hands. "I promise this isn't some sort of orchestrated attempt to spend the night together."

He was cute and friendly and interesting to talk to. The problem was, he wasn't Maeve. He didn't make her heart beat a little faster in her chest whenever she saw him, and she didn't get excited learning all of the little mundane, inconsequential things that made him tick. And that became painfully obvious when he sat down in front of her, and all she thought about was whether Maeve had seen him.

"I didn't think that," she lied. "It's a good bar, but I'm biased. What can I get you?"

A minute later, after she'd sent Jack back to his table, she extracted herself to grab a few minutes of air. She gave Pete a nod on her way out, but she didn't see Maeve.

"Air was a bad idea," she hissed under her breath soon after she opened the back entrance. She turned around quickly, pulling the door behind her at the same time she collided with a body.

"Ooof." Maeve's high groan echoed through the small hallway and sent shivers down Bianca's spine.

She loved being close to Maeve, even if she did feel a little guilty about knocking the wind out of her. Instinctively, Bianca's arms came up to steady her. "You okay?"

She felt Maeve lean into the touch for the briefest moment before her spine straightened. "I'm good. Just wasn't expecting you to turn like that."

Bianca missed the feeling of Maeve's weight against her, their bodies connected in the darkened hallway. "How's your night going?" she asked, keeping her arms wrapped loosely around Maeve's hips.

"How's Jack?" The unmistakable tone of annoyance threaded through Maeve's words.

Was it wrong that Bianca kind of liked it? She intertwined her fingers behind Maeve's back, tightening her hold. She didn't care what it looked like, only how Maeve felt about it. "Is this okay?"

"Depends on whether I need to cover for you at midnight while you sneak off for a kiss."

Bianca's eyes raked across Maeve's features, an ache tugging low in her stomach. This was it. The moment that Bianca knew could change everything between them. Like she'd done on Christmas Eve, she leaned forward and brushed their noses together, willing herself to be brave. When she pulled back, she looked into Maeve's bright blue eyes. "Only if you'll be sneaking off with me."

* * *

Maeve thought she'd gotten over caring what other people thought about her. But as she poured the last drink before midnight, last call in effect, she was vibrating with nervous energy. Because Bianca goddamn Rossi had basically propositioned her to steal a kiss at midnight.

How was she supposed to respond to that? At the time, she'd put all of her maturity on display by pretending it was absolutely urgent that she get back to the bar as soon as possible. She'd eased herself out of Bianca's arms, hating how cold the air felt away from her touch.

The revelry of New Year's Eve had kept her busy, but she was twenty minutes from the countdown, and it was like she could actually hear a clock ticking in her mind.

Fifteen minutes. Bianca had cleared her own line, and she was turning away stragglers with an efficiency that both impressed Maeve and turned her on. Maeve knew this because for the last hour, any second spent not tending to her own job was spent sneaking glances in Bianca's direction, wondering if this was all a dream.

Ten minutes. The bar was split in the focus of their drunken excitement, half of the groups lost in their own world, the other half intently staring at the two television screens behind the bar that usually played sporting events and were now showing the countdown.

Five minutes. Maeve had to make a decision. She was usually better at these. Talking was hard, but action was easy. Except that when Bianca was involved, she forgot everything she'd ever known.

Because Bianca had the broadest smile. And the strongest hands. And the softest... everything.

What was Maeve doing again?

Right, she was putting little signs up along the bar that

Cuffing Season

service was closed. When she placed the last one down, she anxiously looked up to find Bianca.

Not that she knew what she was going to do, but it didn't matter because Bianca was nowhere to be found.

She scanned the crowd. Kelly had left hours ago, and Sawyer and Quinn, whom she'd talked to earlier, had also absconded.

Must be nice to have someone to go home and cuddle up with. That thought stopped Maeve short, intensely enough that she dropped her hand down on the bar so hard the sensation reverberated through her arm.

Where was Bianca? Maeve looked across the crowd but didn't find her in the sea of bodies. She hoped that Bianca hadn't gone off to find Jack. He seemed nice, but fuck that guy.

Moving around the bar quickly, she did another scan of the main room before she walked down the back hallway. Bianca wasn't in the supply room. Or her dad's office. The small area where they kept their jackets was also empty, though Bianca's wasn't on her usual hook.

"Dammit, Bianca," Maeve muttered as she grabbed her own jacket. A second later, she was fighting every instinct she had and pushing the back door open into frigid winter air.

Bianca was there, like Maeve knew she'd be for reasons she couldn't quite explain, leaning against the brick wall a few feet from the door. Her breath was coming out in visible puffs, the below-freezing temperatures making it look like she was smoking a cigarette.

"I didn't know if you'd come."

Maeve stepped up in front of her, close but not touching. "You didn't make it easy. I didn't know where you'd gone."

Everything felt electric when Bianca reached out and wrapped her fingers around the lapel of Maeve's coat, pulling their bodies together, separated by way too much clothing.

Bianca's bright, magnetic eyes drew Maeve in just as much as her physical touch. "I figured you'd head to your usual clandestine makeout spot."

Her hand came up to rest on Bianca's hip, just under the hem of her bulky coat. "That was one time."

"Well, I've certainly thought about it a lot." Bianca dropped the words between them like a ticking bomb.

Maeve groaned and inched closer, willing her erratic heartbeat to slow down. "Oh yeah?"

Bianca let out a soft sigh that Maeve felt through her entire body. "You just seemed so content. A little mischievous, too. I liked it. And I couldn't help thinking about what it would have been like if it was me with you instead of that woman."

Dazed by Bianca's honest words, Maeve didn't process her own hands shifting under Bianca's jacket and settling against her hips, only a thin, black T-shirt separating her hands from Bianca's skin. And god, it felt good. Not just because it was a beautiful woman against her, but because it was *Bianca*.

She felt a little bit desperate when Bianca shifted impossibly closer, her bright green eyes tracking across Maeve's features. Inside the bar, she could make out the faint roar of the countdown.

There was nothing she wanted more than to kiss Bianca at midnight. This was how she wanted to start her year, full of possibility—and maybe a little promise.

* * *

Bianca loved how Maeve fit in her arms. Her hands had traveled under Bianca's T-shirt, but all the cold of Maeve's fingertips did was excite her, make her yearn to get closer.

So she did.

When the sound from the crowd inside grew chaotic,

Bianca leaned forward and, doing something she'd fantasized about dozens of times over the last few weeks, pressed her lips against Maeve's.

Her stomach twisted as Maeve responded to the kiss, drawing Bianca's bottom lip between her own. Maeve's hands slid up Bianca's back, her nails playing lightly up and down her spine, urging them closer together.

A soft sound escaped the back of Maeve's throat, like she was just as affected by the kiss. And then Bianca's knees buckled when she felt Maeve's tongue asking for entry, the insistent tug in her center coiling tighter.

She felt Maeve's thigh ease between her own, pushing her fully back against the wall. Their tongues tangled together, and Bianca's arms wrapped around Maeve's smaller frame as she tried to pull her closer, to find the friction she desperately sought.

It was more than she'd thought it would be, how Maeve's lips were purposeful yet exploratory, gently sucking and nipping in a way that made it impossible for Bianca to think about anything except this moment.

Bianca wasn't sure when her hands had moved up to Maeve's neck, cupping her face gently like she was afraid she'd disappear. That she'd wake up and realize this had all been a vivid dream.

The feeling of loss struck her acutely when Maeve placed one last, sweet kiss against her lips. She leaned back and looked at Bianca, an earnest intensity in her eyes. But Bianca didn't want to overthink things, given that Maeve was literally—and maybe figuratively—pulling away from her.

Maeve's soft voice calmed a little of the nervousness that had settled in her stomach. "I need to get back inside. I feel like I've already left Pete to fend for himself for too long."

Right. Maeve, who alway did the right thing, even when

she was acting like an angry little Tasmanian devil.

"That's fair," Bianca finally responded, dropping her hands down from Maeve's face to rest loosely on her hips. She missed their skin-on-skin contact. And because she was a glutton for punishment, she asked the question that had been on the tip of her tongue since the kiss had started. "So, do you feel like your new year is starting off right?"

"I think it's pretty clear from the way I can't drag myself away right now, even though they could be burning down the bar inside, that I'm officially cuffed." Maeve smiled, and Bianca knew her whole face lit up when she saw the dimple in Maeve's cheek as she added, "If that's what you want."

Chapter Sixteen

Shirley's hand came down to rest on one of the bars of the chest press machine, blocking Maeve's range of motion. "If you pull any harder, you're going to injure yourself."

Over the weekend, Maeve's excitement at a world of possibility had morphed into anxiousness. Things with Bianca had changed. They'd both had a hand in it, she could admit that, but where did they go now?

Maeve had never been great at talking about her feelings. In other news, water was wet.

She was supposed to go over for their now regular Monday movie night, except there was a giant, kiss-shaped elephant in the room that had her feeling more than a little unsteady. It wasn't that she was afraid of it happening again. She was afraid of what it meant.

The days, though still wintry and dreary, seemed a little brighter, which she knew was factually impossible as they entered into January. At the bar this past weekend, she'd even slightly enjoyed the banal chatter that enveloped the small space. Before, it had seemed suffocating. Now? It felt homey, like she'd stumbled onto the set of *Cheers* and honesty didn't mind that everyone knew her name. Her frantic, singular desire to claw her way back to New York City was slowing to an almost afterthought of a crawl, which she could finally admit had been happening for weeks now.

And her heart... well, it did this annoying little pitter-patter whenever she thought about Bianca, when she thought about the next time they'd see one another.

Bianca Rossi had her spinning out, and she wasn't really sure which way was up anymore.

Shirley's hand moved from the bar into Maeve's peripheral vision, and she waved it back and forth a few times. "Did I lose you there?"

Maeve placed the machine back into its resting position and leaned her head back. "Sorry. I just have a lot on my mind."

"Anything I can help with?" Shirley looked surprisingly sympathetic, which wasn't her tone in their normal exchanges.

Maeve briefly considered holding her emotional ground and brushing Shirley's attempt at help off, but she needed someone to talk to. "I was going for no complications during my trip to Kingsford."

"And?"

"I may have stumbled into a complication."

Shirley eyed her seriously. "Care to elaborate? You're going to need to get better at talking about your feelings, kid."

"I'm twenty-eight. I'm not a kid." She didn't know why her annoyance flared. Shirley was always referring to her as some version of a not-yet-adult.

"With the emotional maturity of a kid, apparently. I just call 'em like I see 'em."

Maeve took a few seconds to dramatically drop her head into her hands and lean forward, like she was trying to get in the tornado drill position they taught in elementary school. She wasn't doing a great job of proving herself as an adult in either of their eyes.

"Fine," she said, finally looking up and meeting Shirley's curious eyes. "I kissed someone on New Year's, and I'm confused about it."

"So, what's the problem?"

How Maeve had ended up bearing her emotionally scattered heart to a seventy-two-year-old at the gym on Monday morning eluded her. "Well, it just seems like a bad decision. I'm leaving Kingsford soon."

"And does this person know that?"

"Yes."

"So it sounds like both of you are going into this with your eyes open, no?"

Maeve wanted to roll her eyes at Shirley's simplification of her problem. "It's just complicated."

"Well, you are an adult," Shirley said, enunciating her last word for impact. "I'm sure you can be honest and communicative to ensure there are no bad feelings when you leave."

"Yeah, but..." Maeve stalled, trying to find the right words. "It seems like a risk that may not be worth taking." She wasn't quite ready to admit that it wasn't someone else's heart she was worried about hurting if this all went poorly.

"It's your decision, but you're not the only one impacted. Maybe have a conversation with this person about it?"

"I'll think about it."

Maeve wasn't lying. She'd done nothing but think about the conversation she and Bianca needed to have since they'd parted ways on Friday. The only problem was that she didn't know what to say. Maeve was feeling more than a little out of her depth. But Shirley was right that there was someone she should be talking about it with, if only she could find the words to do it.

* * *

On Monday afternoon, Bianca decided to take lunch out of the office so she could meet Jonny after his New Year's Eve weekend in the city. And maybe because she had a few things she needed to discuss with him.

Bianca smirked at him over her coffee mug. "You look like you're still hungover."

"I am hungover. Yesterday on the train home I'm pretty sure I was still drunk." Gone was his usually polished demeanor as he bit into a bagel sandwich as big as his face.

"Seems like it was worth it, then?"

He shrugged and took another bite. "It was fun. One of those 'do it for the story' weekends, I suppose. How was your weekend? How was work?"

"Eventful."

Jonny lifted a manicured brow. "Do tell."

"Jack was in on New Year's Eve."

"Not where I was expecting this story to go given our previous conversation, but sure."

Bianca rolled her eyes playfully. "I said hi to him, but that was it. I think Maeve maybe got a little jealous?" She said it like a question, even though she knew that was exactly what had happened.

"And how'd that play out? Did she go all sullen?"

Bianca still got tingly all over when she thought about just how not sullen Maeve had been with her outside the bar. "Not exactly."

"Way to bury the lede, Rossi. Come on, spill." She felt Jonny nudging her shoe under the table.

She wanted to. God, she wanted to. But finding the words to encompass how that kiss with Maeve had made her feel was a little daunting. With the first kiss behind them, knowing that Maeve had wanted it too, she looked back on the buildup to it like an extended amount of foreplay, her feelings and her libido way beyond where they should have been given that she'd only kissed someone once.

"We kissed."

"And?"

"What do you mean 'and'?"

"I just figured with all the tension, you'd have taken her home with you." Jonny paused before looking at her seriously. "Or was it not good?"

She resisted laughing in his face at the absurdity of that statement. She could still feel their kiss days later. "Oh, no. It was good. Better than I thought it would be, if that's even possible."

"Then what's the problem? Why are you reverting back to eighth-grade dance rules?"

Bianca let out a strangled sigh. "Well, we agreed there's something between us. We just didn't exactly agree on what that is."

"As in you haven't talked about it or you disagree on what's going on?" She didn't answer, and he finished off his sandwich and gestured vaguely around the room. "And if it's the former, when will you be discussing these finer points?"

"Maybe tonight?" Bianca said, knowing nervousness had seeped into her tone. "From Maeve's reaction, I got the sense that she would be open to pursuing something while she's here. I just have no idea how long that will be. I don't know if she does either."

"That bagel was heavenly," Jonny said as he let out an indulgent sound of satisfaction. "I am coming back to life, which means that I can now offer proper advice."

"Great. My hungover best friend has enough food in him to

actually be functional. I cannot believe people trust you with their money."

"Besides the point. But what I'm hearing is that you're going to compromise on everything you want and Maeve gets exactly what suits her. Is that correct?"

Bianca could not believe him. "You told me to go for this!"

"And I still think that was the right call. All I'm saying is that you need to be prepared for the fact that she's leaving. Are you going to keep dating Jack, too?"

"I called Jack yesterday and told him I wasn't really available anymore."

Jonny slapped his hand against his forehead. "Jesus, Mary, and Joseph."

"I'm not good at juggling people! You know this about me." Bianca lowered her voice and looked at Jonny earnestly, hoping he could understand her next words. "Have you ever met someone and you just felt like it was supposed to happen? That's how I feel about meeting Maeve. I know nothing may come of it, but I can't seem to sit idly by."

"That feels… big." He pulled his hands apart and made an explosion sound for extra, albeit unnecessary, emphasis.

Bianca shrugged to take some of the weight off her statement. She wasn't oblivious to the excellent point Jonny was making, but she also couldn't really explain it. Maeve got under her skin far more than anyone she'd ever met, especially in such a short amount of time. Whether it worked out or not, she'd always wonder what would have happened if she didn't see things to their inevitable—or cataclysmic—conclusion.

"I'm not throwing my rules out the window. I'm just… amending them."

Jonny looked at her for a few seconds before he sat back in his chair. He clasped his fingers behind his head and let out a low whistle. "That must have been some kiss."

Cuffing Season

Bianca felt sparks shoot down her spine at the memory. "You have no idea."

* * *

Maeve didn't have time to knock on the front door of Bianca's house before it opened. And just like that, with Bianca in front of her, all of the confusion and trepidation melted into a buzzy excitement that she was in Bianca's space, breathing the same air. She was so excited, in fact, that she forgot to get out of the freezing cold.

"Are you trying to make some kind of point by standing outside?" Bianca asked, shooing Maeve lightly into the warmth.

Maeve walked inside and slipped her beanie off her head, willing herself to hold on to the excitement instead of letting the other emotions blurring around the edges come back to center stage. She'd promised herself she was going to be more honest. "You just look really pretty. I got distracted."

Bianca blushed, seemingly pleased, and Maeve felt warmth flutter through her own body. "That was a really good answer."

Maeve took off her jacket and hung it by the door before slipping off her boots. Standing up a little straighter, she cleared her throat. "I, um... I wondered if you wanted to talk. About Friday? Or anything really?"

It was hard to read Bianca's face, but her lips were slightly upturned, like she was mostly amused by Maeve's terrible attempts at communication. "I'm impressed. Taking the bull by the horns and all that."

"I know. Not my usual style. But I was talking with Shirley—"

"Like Shirley from the gym? That Shirley?" Bianca interjected, her lips now pulled into a wide smile.

God, all Maeve could think about was kissing her again. "Yes?"

"Just making sure that we were talking about your gym buddy." Bianca pointed to the kitchen. "Do you want some hot cocoa?"

"Sure. Do you need help?"

"I'm pretty proficient in my hot beverage preparation, but sure." Bianca gestured toward Maeve to follow her into the kitchen.

Bianca moved around the small room gracefully, setting a kettle on the stove to boil and pouring two hot cocoa packets into mugs that had become synonymous with "theirs."

It almost seemed like Bianca didn't want to talk, given how she'd shrugged off Maeve's first attempt and was now flitting around the kitchen like putting their drinks together was the most important task of her life.

Being fidgety was Maeve's thing, and it threw her off to feel the nervousness radiating from Bianca. Finally, when she felt like Bianca was close to whittling her own spoons to mix their drinks, she moved next to her.

"You okay?"

"I know we need to talk." Maeve didn't love hearing that, even if she'd suggested it.

Maeve leaned against the counter next to the stove and crossed her ankles. "So let's talk."

The inscrutable look Bianca gave her wasn't helping. They'd both liked what had happened. And ideally, Maeve would like for it to happen again.

When the kettle whistled, Bianca picked it up and began pouring the boiling water between the cups. "I know you're not staying in Kingsford."

Maeve nodded, trying to keep her face neutral. "I know you know that."

Cuffing Season

"But I also like spending time with you." Maeve's little grinch heart felt like it grew three sizes with Bianca's words.

"I like spending time with you too." It was easily the most truthful thing she'd ever said. The idea of not spending time with Bianca anymore, a stability in her life she'd come to rely on, was unfathomable.

"So I guess what I'm saying is that I know you're leaving but I still want this. Want to spend time with you until you do."

Bianca looked at her with wide, unblinking eyes before sliding one of the cocoa cups a few inches toward Maeve.

"I want to spend time with you too," Maeve said quietly, finding it hard to meet Bianca's stare again. It wasn't because she didn't mean the words. It was because of *just how much* she meant them.

She loved how Bianca's lips tipped into a small smile while she stared at her own cup, her long fingers wrapped around its warmth. "Yeah?" she asked, finally lifting her focus.

As their stares met, Maeve felt like a teenager with her first crush, the butterflies tumbling in her stomach. She would do anything to keep that smile on Bianca's face. "Yeah. I think we've been pretty honest with one another. I'm staying for at least a few more weeks so..."

She'd been trying to find a way to broach this topic with Bianca, a decision she'd only come to over the weekend. And it wasn't just because of their fledgling connection, though it would be a lie to pretend like that didn't have something to do with it. She liked working with Sawyer, and the conversation she'd had with her dad had left its mark in ways she hadn't expected. Their relationship had gotten better over the last few days, and more than anything, she was curious to see where it went.

With her mom gone, walking away from her last parent as he'd extended her a tenuous olive branch felt wrong. And not wrong in the "it would make her a bad daughter" way, but wrong like she'd be giving up a chance she didn't know she'd get again. Her mom had been taken so suddenly, so unexpectedly, that any notions about having all the time in the world had been stripped away with a single phone call.

Seven months ago, the worst thing that had ever happened to her had come to pass. The idea that some measure of good could come out of it was something Maeve still hadn't quite processed but didn't want to lean away from.

Maeve scanned Bianca's face for any indication about how she felt to learn that Maeve was staying longer than expected.

When Bianca didn't respond, Maeve ran her finger along the rim of her cocoa cup and asked, "Does that change anything for you?"

Maeve got her answer, but not with words at first. Bianca dipped her head and captured Maeve's lips in a soft kiss. Her pulse fluttered rapidly when Bianca's tongue slid against her bottom lip, and she nipped at it gently before pulling back. "That's great news."

"So we can just do what we've been doing I guess? Maybe with more cuddling?" A world where Maeve was suggesting hanging out and watching a movie while wrapped up in one another's arms wasn't one she'd ever expected to find herself in. She barely recognized herself.

Bianca pushed a lock of hair behind Maeve's ear and gave her another quick kiss. "That sounds perfect."

* * *

It was strange that they were pretending like they had all the time in the world. At least, that was how it felt to Bianca. Things were progressing much slower tonight than she'd expected, given all the thoughts she'd had about Maeve over the last few weeks.

She didn't know if it was better or worse that instead of a sex-fueled night, they found themselves on the sofa, Bianca's head on Maeve's lap as they watched a movie.

Maeve's fingers skimmed gently along her scalp. "Your hair is just as soft as I thought."

Bianca lifted her head and twisted her torso to see Maeve's face. "You've thought about my hair?"

Maeve rolled her eyes but kept her fingertips against Bianca's head. "Yes."

Bianca lay back down, a pleased smile on her face. "I like that you did that."

She didn't want to dig into how normal this whole situation felt, how their relationship had easily slid into one of familiarity and comfortable touches. It was like once they'd admitted something was happening between them, the rest was falling into place.

And knowing that they had more time, weeks longer than Bianca had expected, made it all the better. When Maeve had arrived, Bianca thought their conversation would center on her leaving, possibly within a few days. She'd thought the kiss on New Year's Eve would be all they had, and while she'd think of it fondly forever, it hadn't seemed like enough.

Maeve's fingers stilled against Bianca's temple. "So I guess we're doing this?"

"Doing what?" Bianca asked as she burrowed her cheek against Maeve's lap, wanting her to resume her touches. "Obviously not massaging my head because you've stopped, which is a true travesty."

"Cuffing season."

Bianca turned from her side onto her back so that she could look up at Maeve. Her blonde hair was tousled, illuminated by the light behind her. And there was that dimple Bianca had already grown to love, alleviating any of her whirring thoughts at where this conversation was going. "You okay with that?"

A gentle finger ghosted along her temple before Maeve's knuckles rested against Bianca's cheek. "Are you okay with that?"

Bianca nodded. "I am. Honestly, I think I got a little wrapped up in the idea of what I wanted, so much so that I started missing out on having experiences."

"So your New Year's resolution is to throw all of that out the window?"

"My New Year's resolution is to stop thinking that I can plan everything. It's not like you're some huge red flag. Maybe what we want is incompatible in the long run, but I'd rather know you now than not know you at all."

"That's a good answer," Maeve said.

Maeve bent her head forward and placed a soft, lingering kiss on Bianca's lips. More than a little charmed by the action, Bianca wrapped her arms around Maeve's neck and deepened the kiss.

Because while Bianca knew she was pushing herself out of her own comfort zone to make this work, so was Maeve. And that meant something to her. She hoped that, even if their time together wouldn't last, it would mean something to both of them.

Chapter Seventeen

On Tuesday morning, Maeve was setting up the shots for the day in Sawyer's antique store when Quinn wandered in. Maeve had only talked to her a few times in passing, when she'd been with Sawyer.

"Morning, Maeve." Quinn looked effortlessly chic in a dark blue blazer and tapered slacks.

She continued moving the smaller pieces into an organization that probably she only understood. "Hey, Quinn."

Quinn leaned against an old fireplace and watched Maeve work. "Heard the good news that you're sticking around for a few more weeks. Sawyer's over the moon."

"It made sense. I like this project, and I don't have anything serious lined up back in New York yet." Not the whole truth, but she was fine with it.

"This town really has a way of throwing all of your best-laid plans to the wind."

Maeve nodded in agreement. "Right. You lived in New York City for a long time."

"I did. I'm thankful for my time there, but I'm also really liking being back in Kingsford."

"And how's it going?" Maeve stood up from where she'd been hunched over her photo subjects and looked at Quinn fully.

A soft smile graced Quinn's face. "It's going really well. Some things are taking a little more adjustment, like my relationship with my mom, but getting Sawyer back and my relationship with Kelly and the girls has made it all worth it."

Maeve didn't know if she'd ever be so comfortable expressing her feelings, especially when it came to love. "I'm glad to hear that."

"How are you doing?" It was a throwaway question that didn't feel casual at all.

"Are you pumping me for information?"

"Information about what?"

"I don't know."

"Why do I need information from you?"

"I don't know."

Quinn took a step forward and ran her fingers along one of the antique clocks that Maeve would be photographing that day. "You remind me a little bit of myself. I blame Sawyer for getting me to start caring about other people's feelings, but all I'm saying is that if you ever want to talk, I'm here. Takes a village and all that..."

Maeve raised a brow. "Except I don't need the town's help to raise a hypothetical baby or whatever that statement was implying."

"No," Quinn responded, shaking her head slowly, "but you've gone through a lot the past few months. Trust me, I know that it can feel easier to shoulder burdens alone."

"Well, we can't all grow up to be warm and fuzzy." There

was no mistaking the clip in Maeve's voice, but Quinn wasn't deterred.

"The reality of the situation is that Bianca likes you and Kelly likes Bianca, and Sawyer and I like Kelly."

"Small towns," Maeve said flippantly. She couldn't stop herself from adding, "And Bianca's an adult. I'm sure she knows what she's doing." Which may or may not have been true. Did either of them really know what they were doing beyond the fact that they wanted to spend more time together? There was no way it could end well, but Maeve couldn't pluck up the willpower to care.

"I'm sure she does. It's you I'm worried about."

Maeve stood up straight, but Quinn still had inches on her. "No need to worry about me."

Quinn let out a surprising laugh. "You're really not doing anything to prove to me we aren't alike. But as a piece of advice, one thing I've learned since coming back is that you have to show up for the people you care about." Quinn gave her an annoyingly knowing look, like she had Maeve all figured out. "But I'll get out of your hair."

Ten seconds later, Maeve was alone in the room, feeling like she'd hallucinated the entire conversation. It had happened so quickly that only now were questions starting to slink into her mind. What exactly did Quinn think was going on between her and Bianca? Obviously there was actually something going on, but they hadn't been public about things. At most, they had probably started to look like friends to anyone outside of their Monday night hangouts.

She'd unknowingly stumbled into some sort of protective den of lesbians (and Kelly) who were treating Bianca like she couldn't handle herself where Maeve was concerned.

If only they'd known that last night it had been Bianca who'd instigated things between them, sitting up and shifting over so that she could straddle Maeve's thighs. And then it had been Bianca who had pulled her into quite possibly the most mind-altering kiss of Maeve's life.

Maeve had wanted to stay. Every atom in her body had protested when she'd pulled their lips apart and looked into Bianca's hooded eyes. She hadn't been prepared for just how much Bianca would make her feel, and she was terrified. Add that to the list of unhelpful emotions that had been whirring through her body for the last twelve hours.

So she'd run her hands down Bianca's forearms and then interlaced their fingers before doing something that was so unlike her. She'd lifted one of their clasped hands and kissed Bianca's knuckles. Because she'd wanted to. Because it was what Bianca deserved. Because she liked how Bianca's body had gone rigid and then slackened as she melted into the gesture.

Maybe it was sending mixed messages to Bianca, but Maeve hadn't been thinking about that at the time. All she'd been considering was the soft scowl on Bianca's face that Maeve wanted to kiss away.

So she'd kissed her knuckles before untangling their other hands and cupping Bianca's jaw. When she'd told her she should probably get going, it was hard to tell which one of them was more upset by the admission.

The little thrill at realizing how much Bianca seemed to want her hadn't abated since she'd left, and her body had been sparking with emotions all morning. Even Quinn's overprotective conversation couldn't hamper her feelings. Maeve didn't care how anyone else felt about the situation; she only cared that Bianca was happy with how things were between them. And except for leaving last night, when Bianca had pushed Maeve up against the doorframe and stolen a long, heated kiss,

Maeve would have said that she was making Bianca Rossi pretty damn happy right then.

In spite of how foreign the slowness and sweetness of their relationship was, it was making Maeve pretty damn happy too.

*** * * ***

Bianca had just gotten home from work when her phone chimed.

Maeve Murphy – 5:12 p.m.
Any interest in takeout tonight?

Maeve Murphy – 5:12 p.m.
If you're free

Bianca Rossi – 5:13 p.m.
Trying to hang out two nights in a row. You're really taking to this whole cuffing thing like a duck to water :)

Maeve Murphy – 5:14 p.m.
Are there rules to this? I wasn't given them.

Bianca Rossi – 5:15 p.m.
No rules except the ones we decide. Come over at six thirty?

. . .

That would give Bianca enough time to hop in the shower and tidy up her house. Throw in a few extra minutes to agonize over Maeve's impending arrival, and she'd be right on time.

Maeve Murphy – 5:15 p.m.
How about the Greek place? If that works let me know what you want.

Bianca Rossi – 5:16 p.m.
I will eat literally anything. Surprise me!

Maeve Murphy – 5:16 p.m.
Famous last words...

Bianca liked this. A lot. Whatever was happening between them, and even if it wasn't built to last, it made her feel more alive than she had in a long time. There was something about knowing Maeve was leaving that took the pressure off, like they could play house with no real long-term consequences.

Who didn't love to be greeted with food at their door while in their comfy lounging clothes, the chill of winter hovering outside?

When Bianca opened the door at six thirty on the dot, Maeve was carrying an inconceivable amount of food in her arms.

"Some type of 'going out of business' sale? All food must go?" Bianca asked as she shut the door behind Maeve and followed her into the kitchen.

After dropping the bags on the counter, Maeve slid her

beanie from her head and ran her fingers through her mussed hair. "I panicked." The helpless, overwhelmed look on her face was possibly the cutest thing Bianca had ever seen.

She walked over and unzipped Maeve's coat. Bianca liked that she could do that now. "Why did you panic?"

"I mean, people don't really mean 'get me whatever' when they say that, right? They always want something but don't want to say it. So then I wracked my brain, trying to remember if we'd talked about this place. And I know you like the eggplant sandwich from the cafe downtown, and I know that you like the tagliatelle with black truffle at Murph's. And you like pepperoni and pickled pepper pizza from Vito's." Maeve finally managed a smile. "That one's easy to remember because of all the alliteration. I suggested the Greek place because it didn't come up, but now I'm thinking I should have suggested something I know you like. Our dads aren't in some sort of feud with them, are they?"

Maeve's eyes went wide, and she sucked in an audible breath. Bianca slid Maeve's coat off her shoulders and draped it over her own arm, ignoring the flutters from Maeve's rapid-fire recitation of every food Bianca had probably ever mentioned. "Zorba's is just newer, so I haven't been there yet. I promise I will like it."

Maeve still looked anguished. "How can you know that if you haven't even tried it?"

Instead of trying to pacify Maeve with words, Bianca dipped her head lower and kissed Maeve's jaw. "I will like it." Another kiss, a little farther down. "Because you brought it." Another kiss, just at the edge of Maeve's lip. "And it was very thoughtful."

Bianca sighed as she connected their lips. She'd missed their softness over the course of the day. Kissing Maeve was like staring at a beautiful sunset, a seemingly static experience that changed in the blink of an eye as the hues shifted and the sun dropped lower in the sky. That was what it felt like when Maeve asked for entry with her tongue at the same time her hands wrapped around Bianca's waist and pulled her closer.

Pleasure washed over Bianca's body when Maeve's fingers skimmed along her torso. When she pulled away to tell Maeve just how good the touch felt, her stomach twisted as she took in the flush blooming across Maeve's cheeks.

Bianca used the hand that wasn't still holding Maeve's coat to brush a loose strand of hair back behind her ear, like she'd seen Maeve herself do many times. "Seems kinda silly how long we waited to start doing that."

Maeve rolled her shoulder into Bianca's chest and nuzzled her nose against her neck. And that caused a whole other set of sparks to shoot through Bianca's body. She loved this soft, playful version of Maeve almost as much as she liked her all broody and mysterious.

When Maeve pulled back, Bianca saw hesitation in her eyes. "What's wrong?"

"I don't even know if it's worth bringing up, but I had some sort of weird, cryptic conversation with Quinn today."

Bianca placed Maeve's coat on the kitchen counter and crossed her arms. "About what?"

"You. Me. Us, I guess?" Maeve shrugged, but Bianca could see the lingering hesitation in her eyes.

It wasn't what Bianca had been expecting to hear, but it also wasn't the most surprising thing in the world. "I haven't mentioned anything to anyone, so this sounds like some misguided sense of trying to protect me and my fragile romantic heart," Bianca said with an eye roll for good measure, though she planned to have a conversation with Kelly about how this conversation had possibly come up.

"Your fragile romantic heart?"

"I know that people think I'm soft."

"I don't think that." Maeve scrunched her nose up, like she was trying to work something out before she admitted, "Actually, maybe I thought that when I first met you, but I don't think that anymore."

"Which is why you get to see the other parts of me too," Bianca said before she dipped her head again and scraped her teeth along Maeve's neck, sucking on warm skin as she dotted kisses along its smooth column.

She liked that she could feel Maeve's pulse flutter against her lips, her hands coming up to wrap themselves into Bianca's hair.

Maeve's voice dropped lower when she said, "If this is what I get for honesty, I will most definitely make it my policy moving forward."

Bianca only moved her lips away so that she could say, "Good," against her neck again before she returned her attention to what she was doing because god, was she enjoying doing it. Maeve smelled like cedar, and it reminded Bianca of being in a log cabin, out of the cold and with the heat radiating from Maeve's body better than any crackling fire.

The consequences be damned, this moment felt worth it. With Maeve in her arms, skin against Bianca's lips, she didn't want to be anywhere else. Didn't want to be doing anything else.

It was the breathy sound that escaped Maeve's lips that tipped the situation from a manageable fire to a raging inferno that spiraled out of Bianca's control. Her center tightened with need, magnified when Maeve's fingers pushed insistently into her hips to pull them together. Bianca had Maeve up against the kitchen counter, her thigh pushing into Maeve's center before she'd processed the movement.

Before this situation went completely off the rails, Bianca

let herself nip at Maeve's skin one last time before she eased her face back, not surprised by the hooded look in Maeve's eyes that she was sure was mirrored in her own. "I know you went to all the trouble of buying everything on the menu, apparently, but are you up for reheating it later?"

It was like those words sparked Maeve back to life, her smile tilting into a lopsided grin, her eyes growing sharp and focused. "I can be amenable to that."

"Good," Bianca said, already pulling at Maeve's shirt. "Can you take this off?"

She didn't give Maeve more than a few seconds before she was tugging her along, down the hallway that led toward her bedroom. She felt like she couldn't wait another literal second to have her hands and lips and tongue on Maeve again.

When they walked in the room, Bianca was already wrestling with Maeve's shirt, made more difficult as her lips found their way to Maeve's collarbone. How she'd thought she could deny this attraction, in spite of the obstacles, seemed insane to think about when she was finally presented with the smooth, clean lines of Maeve's stomach. She wanted to lick her abs... among other places.

Maeve's hands moved up to Bianca's long-sleeved thermal, and she coaxed Bianca's lips away from her chest long enough to remove it too. Right, both of them naked. God, that was going to feel amazing.

She slipped out of her joggers and unfastened her bra while she watched Maeve take off her jeans.

"I thought about you in my bed," Bianca said, which made Maeve stutter-step in the cutest way, like she was surprised to hear that information. "You've got to know that, right? How much I want you?" Bianca took a step forward and trailed her fingers along Maeve's toned stomach, just above the waistband of her underwear, loving how the muscles clenched under Bianca's light touch.

"Bianca." Maeve's voice was half warning, half wanting as she wrapped her hands into Bianca's hair again and pulled their lips together.

She loved the way Maeve kissed, like her lips and her face were something to be revered, to be lauded like a gift instead of just a quirk of lucky evolution. A lot of people told Bianca she was pretty, but Maeve made her *feel* it, and that was making all the difference as heat coiled low in her stomach.

When she had Maeve backed up to the bed, she pushed her down gently with both hands, holding them against her shoulders once Maeve was finally seated.

Maeve's hands stroked along Bianca's hips before she trailed them up to her chest. When she ran her fingers along Bianca's nipples, already aching with need, her voice was low and slow when she said, "You're gorgeous."

She needed more. All she'd been fantasizing about since last night was fucking Maeve senseless and cuddling her after. It was exactly like Jonny had said, only he was wrong about who wanted to do it.

"Scoot back?" Bianca said, aware of the predatory look in her eye as she followed Maeve across the bed.

And then she was on top of Maeve, skin on skin and so deliciously hot that the ache in her center grew to a desperate tug. It intensified when she slid her leg between Maeve's and heard how her breath caught when she pushed into her.

"Fuck," Maeve said as Bianca ground against her, unable to stop the intensity building through her body that was flowing out through her hips.

Bianca had always loved sex. Her taste in partners and frequency had changed over the years, but there was nothing better than that catch of connection taking hold as you worked together, building the moment into a frenzy that took on a life of its own.

Yeah, she liked that a lot, and she wanted to feel it with Maeve.

"What do you like?" she asked before licking the shell of Maeve's ear.

Maeve let out a strangled laugh as her hands came up to anchor Bianca's hips in place and create more friction. "You grinding on top of me is quickly moving to the top of the list."

"Good because I'm getting a hell of a lot out of it too." Her long breaths turned into shorter pants as she leaned in and stole a messy, heated kiss.

She was always enthusiastic, but this level of wantonness was new, even for her. Maybe it was the expiration date looming over their relationship, but she wanted to make Maeve feel everything, to leave an imprint that they'd never forget.

Her hips strained against Maeve's when she felt a hand snake between them, a dexterous finger already circling around her clit. "I'm not sure I expected you to be so aggressive," Maeve said as she matched Bianca's rhythm with her fingers.

She was already close as another wave of desire slid down her spine. A few more well-placed strokes from Maeve would send her toppling over the edge. Leaning down, she bit Maeve's earlobe and tangled one of her hands through Maeve's hair, pulling lightly to expose her neck. "I'm a simple woman. I'll fuck you senseless with a strap-on and then happily have the favor repaid," Bianca said breathlessly into Maeve's ear.

Maeve's muscles clenched, like she'd turned to stone, before her legs bowed outward and Bianca slid farther between them, riding Maeve's fingers as her own orgasm overtook her. It was every bit as hot as Bianca had imagined. The way Maeve's free hand had come around to grab Bianca's ass and pull her in tighter. The moan that came out of Bianca's mouth that she wouldn't have been able to stop even if she'd wanted to.

And then, unexpectedly, as she came down, Maeve moved the hand on Bianca's ass up higher, her fingers rubbing lightly up and down her spine.

"So that was..."

"Yeah," Maeve answered.

"And we have..."

"Insane chemistry."

Bianca burrowed her head into Maeve's neck and inhaled that cedar scent again, now slightly masked with sweat. She didn't care. She wanted to remember everything about this moment.

* * *

An hour later, Maeve found herself sitting up in Bianca's bed with a tray of reheated Greek food between the two of them. She was wearing a pair of shorts and a t-shirt that Bianca had given her, feeling all kinds of comfy and blissed out.

She hadn't had sex like what they'd just done in a long time —maybe ever. Enthusiastic and tender and hot and hitting a million notes in between, Maeve was sated, a pleasant ache in her limbs that only came with her toughest workouts anymore.

Her brain, for once, was calm as she scooped baba ganoush onto her pita.

"So, Kingsford..." Bianca asked before she popped a dolma in her mouth.

It took a few seconds for Maeve to process Bianca's words. She looked over at Bianca, chewing thoughtfully while she waited for Maeve to answer. "What about it?"

"You don't seem to like it here all that much. Any reason why?" Bianca had put her sex-mussed hair up in a ponytail, and she sat cross-legged facing Maeve while they both picked food from the tray.

"I like being in your bed right now very much. I think this counts as me liking Kingsford." She flashed a lop-sided smile at Bianca, noticing the slight discoloration on her neck from where she'd sucked harder than she'd thought. But really, Bianca had an amazing neck.

Bianca rolled her eyes. "You know what I mean."

Maeve busied herself with scooping more dip on her pita. In spite of what they'd just done together, it's not like she expected Bianca to understand. She wasn't going to give a real answer, that is, until she looked up again and saw Bianca's face, earnest and open in a way that made Maeve feel like the words were being pulled out of her regardless of whether she wanted to say them or not. "I was the weird kid. I didn't have friends, and that made me an easy target growing up. I don't have a lot of great memories associated with this town."

A little crease appeared between Bianca's brows. "Kids are unnecessarily cruel. It's like a ladder. Even the weak will bully the weaker just to make sure they aren't on the bottom rung."

"I'm not weak."

Bianca was already leaning across the tray between them, on her knees as she ghosted a quick kiss across Maeve's lips. "I know, babe. I just meant that regardless of the pecking order, a lot of kids can be assholes."

"Easy to see the view from the top," Maeve said without thinking.

The look Bianca gave Maeve was arresting in the worst way, like she'd just disappointed her. The happy, grin from seconds ago was replaced with a slight frown, Bianca easing herself back down into a sitting position. "My nickname for the first three years of high school was 'Bobble Head Bianca' because I was tall and gangly and hadn't grown into my features yet."

"Oh."

Quietly, Bianca added, "And I felt like you didn't see me as someone who judged other people in that way."

Well, she'd fucked this up royally. "I'm sorry. You're right and that was unfair."

Bianca lifted a skeptical eyebrow. "If you go looking for the worst in people, you'll probably find it. Same is true with assuming their intentions."

Maeve cleared her throat, willing the churning in her stomach to go away. To make that look on Bianca's face go away. "I know. I've never been very good at talking to people. And you're right, I do assume what other people are thinking. My shitty adolescent experience is no reason to carry a chip on my shoulder, and it's especially not an excuse to put that on other people."

She waited, watching as Bianca absorbed her words, wondering if she'd accept them. Maeve wondered if she herself really accepted them until she'd said them out loud. But Maeve did make a lot of assumptions about people. And she did always expect to find the worst. Her default setting didn't skew toward positive, and she spent most of her time waiting for people to disappoint her. It hadn't gotten her where she'd wanted to go, so maybe a new outlook wouldn't be the worst thing.

Finally, Bianca's lips tipped into a small smile, and it felt like the world had righted itself. "You're unfairly cute when you look like that."

"Like what?" Maeve asked, genuinely confused but latching onto the small kernel of hope in her chest at Bianca's change in tone.

"Like you were worried you'd disappointed me." And then, excruciatingly slowly, Bianca leaned forward on her knees again, stopping to give Maeve a pointed stare before stealing another kiss.

"I feel like you're rewarding bad behavior," Maeve said a little breathlessly when Bianca pulled her lips away.

Bianca shook her head. Her stare dropped down to Maeve's lips before she dragged her gaze up to meet Maeve's eyes. "Not at all. I'm giving you another kiss because you told me something that I'm sure was hard for you to admit. I like people that try. I find it very, very sexy." Bianca stole a glance at the clock on her end table. "Are you done with dinner? I'm suddenly hungry for something else."

The erratic thrum from Maeve's pulse settled in her center as she watched Bianca grab the tray and slide off the bed effortlessly. She walked it over to the dresser and deposited it before turning on her heels and licking her lips as her stare tracked over Maeve's body.

There was no doubt about it. Bianca Rossi could read her like a book. But for the first time in her life, Maeve didn't mind it at all.

Chapter Eighteen

Bianca had spent the last few days more distracted than any time in recent memory. It wasn't difficult to pinpoint the source of her preoccupied thoughts on this particular Friday morning. Maeve Murphy had ignited something in her, a craving that made it hard for Bianca to focus on anything except how good it had felt to be with her on Tuesday night. Better than she'd even thought, and she'd thought about it a lot.

Which is why, when she finally heard someone clear their throat from the other side of the front desk, her head shot up in surprise as she put on her most congenial smile, gearing up to apologize.

Except, she knew for sure the person standing across from her didn't have an appointment. "Maeve? What are you doing here?"

They'd been texting all morning, through Maeve's workout at the gym and then as she'd gotten ready to head to Sawyer's to continue her project. But now, like Bianca had manifested her with sheer fantasy, Maeve was looking at her with that cute little smirk, wearing the same coat she'd had on when they'd kissed on New Year's Eve.

"I brought you a coffee and a scone." She slid the paper cup and small pastry bag a few inches closer to Bianca.

Bianca snuck a glance around the waiting room. There was only one person in the far corner, and all the techs were busy with appointments. She stretched out her hand and picked up the coffee. Maeve's bright blue eyes tracked the movement. "A reward for a job well done?" Bianca asked, dropping her voice to almost a whisper.

A flush wrapped itself around Maeve's neck that gave Bianca a little thrill to be the one to cause it. Maeve eased her forearm forward and leaned closer. "You said you were tired today and..." Maeve bit at the inside of her cheek before settling on her words. "Well, I know you have to work tonight, so I wanted to bring you a little pick-me-up. Is that okay?"

With a nod, she kept her stare focused on Maeve. She picked up the cup and took a sip before running her tongue around the edge of the rim to grab a few stray droplets of coffee. "Absolutely."

She saw heat flare in Maeve's eyes. There was nothing she could do about the desire that settled low in her own stomach except enjoy its presence, in spite of the timing.

Seconds of silence passed between them, both just staring across the desk at one another, Bianca sure she could draw Maeve's lips from memory at this point. Until finally, Maeve cleared her throat, like she remembered where they were. She leaned back and stood up straight, picking up her own coffee cup. "Well, I've got to get over to Sawyer's for a few hours before the bar, but I'll see you later?"

Bianca managed to acquiesce with a head tilt while she tried to find her words, finding it more than a little difficult to form a

Cuffing Season

coherent thought. With a soft exhale, she dropped her stare down to Maeve's lips for one more indulgent look before dragging her focus back up to Maeve's eyes. "Yes. You'll definitely see me later."

When she finally heard the door close behind Maeve, she let out a long breath and leaned back in her chair. The unexpected laugh behind her cut through the din of want and made Bianca shoot upright.

"Wow," Kelly said, still laughing as she moved from the hallway into the reception area. "That was... something."

Now it was Bianca's turn to blush. "She was dropping by with some coffee since I'm working at the bar tonight." She held up the coffee cup, like it proved her point.

"Sure."

Kelly's interest reminded Bianca of her conversation with Maeve on Tuesday. Whatever she'd just seen between the two of them probably wasn't going to help her next words. "Did you know Quinn talked to Maeve?"

"Hmmm...." Kelly said noncommittally.

"Kelly." She knew the sharpness she wanted to infuse in her voice came out softer than a butter knife.

"What? None of us are blind. Sawyer's thought there was something going on between you two forever. Looks like she was right about the interest but wrong about the timeline."

"It's not like that."

"Oh, please. Maeve was just standing in this waiting room, looking at you like a present she'd already unwrapped before and was just dying to unwrap again."

Bianca wondered if her face could flush anymore, and she pulled at the neck of her t-shirt to get a little circulation. "Well, whatever is going on, I don't need you guys meddling."

Kelly grew contrite. "I'm sorry. I didn't mean to overstep. I just care about you, and I may have mentioned that it seemed like you and Maeve were getting closer. What Sawyer and Quinn took away from that is all them."

It was hard to be annoyed when Kelly looked so sincere. "I mean, yes, something is going on, but it's not serious. Which we're both on the same page about," Bianca said resolutely. "I know she's leaving. We're just having fun."

"Famous last words for queer women in Kingsford."

Bianca rolled her eyes. "Maeve and I aren't Sawyer and Quinn."

If soulmates existed, Sawyer and Quinn were that for one another. She didn't know what she and Maeve were. All she knew for certain is that she liked when Maeve was close, how she was curious to explore both Maeve's body and her mind, for however long she could.

Kelly took a step forward and wrapped her hand around Bianca's. "I know. I just don't want to see you get hurt."

The sentiment was sweet, if not a little misplaced. "I appreciate that, but we've talked about the constraints of this thing between us. Neither has false ideations."

Kelly nodded slowly, her face not giving anything away. "I guess I just thought that she'd be leaving by this time."

It's not like that thought hadn't flitted through Bianca's mind, but between the work Sawyer had given her and Maeve working on mending fences with her dad, which she'd told Bianca about on Tuesday, she figured that Maeve was staying where the water was warm. Considering another possibility wasn't a good idea for either one of them.

"She's still working out logistics for her return. She gave up her apartment when she came home, along with the freelance projects she was working on."

"Makes sense," Kelly answered, wrapping her knuckles softly on the desk before looking toward the waiting room. "Well, I'm ready for Mr. Benson and Kodiak now."

Left alone in the waiting room, Bianca leaned back in her chair and took a sip of the coffee Maeve had brought, fixed just the way she liked it.

Bianca had always felt confident when she said she had things under control, but with the taste of coffee and missed kisses lingering on her lips, she hoped that she was right this time.

* * *

On Friday night, Maeve was setting up her bar station, ready for the evening crowd when her dad stepped through the swinging doors with a box of liquor bottles.

"I'm not sure if you realize how many more bottles we've been going through than normal," he said, placing the box on top of the bar. He started to shelve the bottles in their places and gave her a genuine smile, one that Maeve had started to see more of over the last week.

She wiped her hands on the towel over her shoulder and scowled at him, though there was no heat behind her eyes. "Worried I'm pouring too heavy?"

"Not at all. I've been through the receipts. Sales are up, and I know it's thanks to the changes you've made around here." He paused for a second before adding, "Not only did you keep things running while I was out of it, but you've made some great improvements."

Maeve was surprised at the tug in her heart at his praise, but she shrugged it off. "It's what anyone would have done."

He turned back toward her and rested his elbow on the almost empty box. "Not many people would take on what you've done the last few months. And even fewer than that would implement a cocktail program and improve our revenue by thirty percent."

She waved him off. "I'm sure that was holiday-fueled more than anything."

"Maeve." When she met his stare, she saw her own eyes reflected back at her, sincerity pooling in their blue depths. "Thank you. I know we haven't discussed when you'll go back to New York City, but I wanted you to know that I'm finally starting to feel like myself again. I still miss your mom like hell, but since we talked a few weeks ago, I've been able to get my priorities back in order. If you want to be in New York City, I want to do whatever I can to support that. And the first thing is finding someone to take over your shifts."

Maeve nodded in understanding, but his words made her stomach churn instead of providing the relief she'd been expecting to feel. This is what she wanted. For her dad to be in a good place emotionally, financially, and physically. To feel like she was absolved of her daughterly duties and free to return to her real life.

Only, this life was starting to feel pretty real too. Morning coffee with her dad, which they'd started doing about a week ago. And her scheduled but without fanfare workouts with Shirley, who was the perfect balance of poignant and sarcastic.

And then there was Bianca, who walked into the bar just as Maeve thought about her, causing her heart to do a stutter-step with the force of how good it felt to see her.

"Hey," Bianca said, waving at both of them as she continued on toward the staff room to put down her jacket and bag.

Schooling the slightly lovesick smile on her face before she looked back at her dad, she popped the lid back on the garnishes she'd prepped and began cleaning the area up. "I appreciate you saying that. I think at this point, I only have a few weeks of work left for Sawyer Kent, so I'd like to finish that project up."

"And then?" her dad asked without expectation.

When she saw Bianca walking out of the hallway into the bar area, all the feelings she was overwhelmed to feel rushing to the surface, she looked at her dad quickly. "Can we talk about specifics at home? I just need to give it some thought."

"Sure," he said, and she thought he snuck a glance at what had captured Maeve's attention, but he could have just been checking the clock above the hallway. "No rush on my side, I just didn't want you to feel like you were putting things off on my account anymore."

Maeve nodded, channeling her restless energy into organizing everything on the bartop within reach. It was hard to pick apart exactly what she was feeling, hearing she'd been given the green light to go. All she knew, because she wasn't completely out of touch with her emotions thanks to Bianca's influence over the past few months, was that getting everything she'd said she wanted wasn't supposed to make her feel like this.

* * *

Bianca watched Maeve click the lock closed behind the last stragglers out of the bar. Tonight had been a little bit torturous. The first night they'd worked side-by-side after sleeping together. Bianca hadn't expected to feel so on edge, frustrated to be thrust from the safety of her house into a world where she couldn't touch or caress or show Maeve all the ways in which she'd been thinking about her tonight.

Maeve had dutifully tended her station, pouring drink after drink like a machine. Bianca had seen the focus and dedication Maeve could apply to other endeavors, and watching her work had taken on a whole new meaning.

Her instinct was to push Maeve against the door and show

her just how much she'd missed her, but she didn't know that it would be appreciated given where they were.

When Maeve walked across the room and pulled out the broom from behind the bar to start sweeping up, Bianca tracked her stare like a predator circling its prey. When had she become so addicted to Maeve's presence? Maybe it was because what they had to give one another was mostly physical that she was like a hungry lion who'd gone too long without a meal.

Except, Maeve gave her a lot more than that, and she knew it. Dimpled smiles and soft caresses and poignant commentary on even the worst movies they watched. Add in the unprompted coffee and scone this morning, and Bianca was feeling more than a little unsteady about their situation. A physical, no strings attached arrangement was quickly blossoming into something more, and Bianca had already said multiple times with determination that she had things under control. Hell, she'd said it to herself after Maeve had left the vet's office earlier today.

She'd finished cleaning up the bar area and was washing her hands, but all she could think about was backing Maeve up against the closest wall—she'd amended her fantasy from the door about thirty seconds ago—and leaving a trail of wet kisses against her warm skin. She loved how Maeve reacted under her touch. For Maeve's prickly exterior, she was so physically reactive that just thinking about it made Bianca wet. The sounds that came out of her perfect lips were something Bianca wanted to keep on a recording to play on lonely nights.

"Bianca?" Maeve's voice jarred Bianca out of the rampant fantasy she'd been caught up in.

"Sorry. What?" She shook her already clean hands and grabbed a paper towel to dry them.

Maeve stood in the middle of the room, her arms wrapped

around the broom. "I finished sweeping, but you should head home if you want."

Were they not going to be them—or at least the 'them' they'd become inside of Bianca's house—if they were here at work? She didn't like that.

Clearing her throat, she stood up to her full height. "Trying to get rid of me?"

"Absolutely not." Maeve gave her an embarrassed smile and shrugged, like she wasn't being thoughtful when she added, "I know you've had a long day."

It was a sweet sentiment, but it wasn't what Bianca wanted. Slipping around the bar, she crossed the open space until she stood in front of Maeve. Finally alone, it was like something had overtaken her, propelled by a force she couldn't restrain. She ran her fingers lightly down the side of Maeve's hip. "Is it okay if I kiss you here?"

She felt like she could almost see Maeve's pulse point thrumming, loving the effect their close proximity was having on both of them. Bianca could feel the blood thrumming through her own body, and she bit her lip in anticipation.

Half a second after Maeve nodded, Bianca had their hands intertwined. She walked Maeve over to the nearest wall, intent on making her fantasy become a reality, at least to whatever extent Maeve was also a willing participant.

"You look so hot tonight," she said, backing Maeve up against the wood paneled wall that she'd never look at the same way again, now that she knew what Maeve looked like pressed up against it.

"Bianca," fell out of Maeve's lips, her voice husky as her hands came up to anchor on Bianca's hips and pull them closer.

And then, Bianca did what she'd been thinking about for hours, dipping her head lower and peppering kisses along Maeve's neck. Her own reaction was matched by Maeve's wandering hands, taking in a sharp breath when Maeve's fingers found their way under Bianca's shirt and scratched across her skin.

Sliding her leg between Maeve's, she eased her flush with the wall. The soft whimper Maeve exhaled caused an ache in Bianca's center, and she pushed their bodies together and shifted her thigh upward.

"So... not tired," Maeve said in a strangled voice that was both wanting and exasperated as Bianca continued to rock her body, Maeve matching her enthusiasm with each thrust.

"Never too tired for this. For you," she added before she shifted her lips to capture Maeve's in a heated kiss. Her tongue matching the tempo of her hips, she pushed their hips together, surprised at her inability to tamp down on her want, more than willing to take things as far as Maeve would let them go.

It hit her like a ton of bricks. Maeve was leaving soon. Actually leaving. They wouldn't see one another on Friday nights to work together. There would be no curling up on the sofa and watching movies. No teasing one another with soft touches until one of them pushed the other into action with just the right caress, tipping the moment over the edge.

This thing between them was so new—but so good—and the possibility of their situation made Bianca's heart flutter at the same time the reality of it made her stomach bottom out.

All the uncertainty did was make Bianca grow more frenzied, wanting to bottle this moment and keep it forever. To experience every touch and taste and sound with Maeve while they still had time.

"Bianca," Maeve groaned when fingertips pushed insistently against her stomach, Bianca's hand dipping below the waistband of her jeans.

The whine that escaped her own lips when Maeve's hands wrapped into her hair and tugged lightly caused them both to freeze, and Bianca looked down into eyes that she was already a little lost in.

"Can I touch you?" Bianca asked, her voice throaty and full with the want that seemed to be leaking out of every pore in her body. Her fingers continued to trace patterns at the edge of Maeve's jeans, dipping again when she made her request.

"Please," she whispered into the air between their mouths before leaning forward to nip at Maeve's bottom lip and slide her tongue across it.

"Baby, yes." Maeve pulled Bianca's face closer and placed a trail of unexpectedly light kisses against her jaw.

The term of endearment lodged in Bianca's heart like a knife. Add in the sweetness of Maeve's touch, how her hand was still loosely wrapped in Bianca's hair, and she knew—a final type of certainty in the inevitability of it all—this thing between them wouldn't end without her getting hurt.

Already, the hurt seemed bigger than she wanted to manage, but what if this went on for weeks longer? What would that hurt feel like? Maybe more than she could handle, knowing that there would be a hole left in her world when Maeve was gone.

If she couldn't tell Maeve, she could show her. Future Bianca's problems were not hers. All she cared about right now was the coldness against her fingertips as she unfastened the button on Maeve's jeans and slid down her zipper in a swift motion, working to get back to the heat waiting for her.

She eased her hand against Maeve's entrance and pushed inward, running her fingers against her opening while bracketing Maeve in place with her thigh. "You feel so good."

"Please," Maeve begged again in a way that Bianca was growing a little addicted to hearing, her fingers tightening in Bianca's hair with the first exploratory strokes.

She eased a single finger inside and curled upward, loving

the wet heat that engulfed her. "Bringing me coffee this morning is definitely behavior worth rewarding."

Maeve groaned when Bianca removed her finger, only to let out a short exhale when she slipped two back inside, pumping gently into the tightness. The slickness enveloped her fingers as Maeve pulled her back into a messy, uncoordinated kiss that left her breathless. Using her thigh as leverage, she pushed up, her fingers going deeper until she curled against the spot she was looking for, Maeve's back arching up from the wall. Their chests brushed together. Bianca's nipples, already sensitive without being touched, ached inside her bra, straining for release.

But this wasn't about her. It was about making Maeve come so hard that any other future lover would be a comparison—not a different experience.

She could feel the breathy sounds coming from Maeve's lips everywhere, and she watched as Maeve tipped her head back against the wall, one hand still in Bianca's hair and the other pulling insistently against her hip, willing their bodies to get closer.

Bianca knew the feeling. When Maeve's leg came up to wrap around her calf, she let out her own involuntary moan as wetness pooled between her legs.

"Oh my god, Bianca." The words were rushed and frenzied, much like the way Maeve's hips moved against her own, looking for friction as Bianca pumped into her, keeping the pace slower to prolong the moment.

How many more times do we get to do this? Bianca thought as she slid her fingers through delicious heat. *How many more times will I get to hear what Maeve sounds like when she falls apart?*

"Do you want to come?" Bianca teased with her words, but

it was her fingers that made Maeve gasp when she brushed her thumb lightly against Maeve's clit.

"Please," Maeve panted.

Bianca loved how Maeve's hand tightened in her hair, how her hips had lost their tempo and were bucking wantonly against Bianca's hand, straining for release.

"Look at me." She knew it was a bad idea, to stare into Maeve's eyes, to map her features and freckles while she came, but the alternative felt impossible. Bianca was on this ride, and she had every intention of taking full advantage, even if the end result would feel worse for her.

Maeve's focus snapped up to Bianca, blue eyes dark and cloudy, her lips parted. Bianca brought her arm up to wrap around the nape of Maeve's neck, pulling their faces inches away from one another.

"You feel so fucking good," she said before kissing Maeve. She captured Maeve's moan and slipped her tongue inside, matching the tempo of her fingers, increasing the pressure on Maeve's clit and circling the hard nub with her thumb. "So good," she said when she broke away as Maeve's walls clenched around her.

Bianca wanted to see her while she felt her, and she wasn't disappointed at the cry that broke free from Maeve's lips, her whole body going rigid against Bianca, who continued to pump against her, lengthening and slowing her strokes to draw the orgasm out.

She nuzzled her nose against Maeve's neck, kissing lightly against the salty skin before she withdrew her fingers slowly.

"Holy shit," Maeve said toward the ceiling, her head tipped back against the wall.

Bianca watched as Maeve's chest rose and fell. Her breathing was evening out, except when she let out a choppy exhale as an aftershock jolted through her.

"Yeah?" She knew her voice had a pleased tone, though it was husky with her own arousal that hadn't been abated. There was an uncertainty in Maeve's eyes that stopped her short. She brought a hand up to Maeve's chin and pulled her focus. "What's wrong?"

"Nothing's wrong," Maeve said, her voice still a little unsteady. "I was just... um... well I know we don't usually hang out on the weekends, but I was wondering if you wanted me to come home with you and repay the favor. Preferably with less clothing."

It doesn't mean anything's changed, Bianca chided herself as a smile worked its way across her face. "That sounds like a perfect way to end my night."

Chapter Nineteen

Maeve's life had fallen into a rhythm over the last two weeks. Monday and Tuesday nights, she would go over to Bianca's house and they'd watch a movie and eat dinner, followed by what Maeve would qualify as the best sex of her life—and it kept getting better.

She hadn't brought up finding a replacement with her dad, though she knew the conversation was long overdue. And she'd stopped sending emails to prospective clients and agencies she'd worked for to inquire about any work.

It's not like she didn't know what she was doing. She absolutely did, but she couldn't seem to stop herself. Being in Kingsford was starting to feel right in a way she'd never imagined, and turning away from that feeling was becoming impossible.

Because really, what was back in New York City for her? No stable job. No apartment. No family. No *person*. And even if there was a person, it wasn't the person she wanted.

The person she wanted was Bianca, who just last night had decided that it would be a waste of a perfectly good opportunity if she didn't handcuff Maeve to the headboard. By the third orgasm, Maeve had begged to be able to touch Bianca back, who'd told her that she could take care of herself, but Maeve was welcome to watch.

And fuck, was that something that would go down in the history books as one of the all time hottest things that had ever happened to Maeve, and she'd thought of little else over the last twenty-four hours.

Staying in Kingsford wasn't something Maeve let herself actively think about. In her mind, staying and not going were two separate things. Right now, she was not going back to New York because of how things were working out. But she hadn't decided to stay. That felt like a big decision, and one that carried more weight than she was prepared to deal with.

Staying in Kingsford meant committing to that idea, and she'd committed to very few things in her life with the exception of getting out of Kingsford and learning photography.

She still had about a week of work left for Sawyer, though new pieces were showing up at the store every day. The antiques that had shown up today alone could add another few days to her schedule if she wanted them, even though Sawyer had told her there was no expectation to do more than the initial work they'd scoped out together.

But why wouldn't she? She liked working for Sawyer. She liked the routine she'd settled into.

For the last ten years, she'd felt like she was pushing and pushing against a wall that never seemed to budge. Making connections. Building her portfolio. Staying in the city where she thought the water was warm for professional growth.

Back in Kingsford for the better part of a year now, and her life was finally starting to feel like it was making sense. If only she could get over where it was happening to be excited that it was happening at all.

She let out a disgruntled sound of frustration before realizing that she wasn't alone in the Victorian-home-turned-antique-store.

"I hope that wasn't on my account." Quinn said, stepping fully into the room. It was clear she was referring to their conversation three weeks ago, which Maeve hadn't handled the best.

"No." Maeve smiled and tucked her hair behind her ear. "I promise it's not. Sawyer ran out to get lunch, but she should be back soon."

Quinn nodded and took a step forward. "Actually, I was hoping to run into you. I wanted to apologize if I upset you in any way the last time we talked. I'm still getting the hang of this whole 'small town' thing, and I didn't mean to overstep any boundaries."

Her apologetic tone seemed sincere, but they stood in the silence until Maeve finally spoke. "I appreciate that. I shouldn't have been..." Maeve struggled to finish her thought, coming up with, "the way I can be sometimes. I'm not always the best at communicating, and I know you were only trying to help."

"Was I though?" Quinn responded, her face breaking into a sheepish grin. "I think you could argue that I was trying to scare you a little bit."

Maeve laughed. "Oh, I got that message loud and clear, I just didn't think it was helpful to bring up."

"Well, you're still here. I wanted to run something by you. If you're open to that?"

"Sure. What's up?"

"I wouldn't have dared poach you from Sawyer, but since you've done the bulk of your project with her, and really well, from what she tells me, I was wondering if you were open to picking up any more work?"

Did she believe in fate? Or did she believe that the devil

works hard, but lesbians work harder–especially if their goal was to keep Maeve in Kingsford for as long as possible.

"What's the job?"

Quinn closed the last few feet of space between them and handed over her business card. "The busy real estate season starts in April. I'd like to get some design collateral in order before then, and I'll need someone to work with me during the spring and summer to photograph the homes going on the market. It's not the most exciting, soul-enriching photography work on the planet, but it will be steady."

Months of work that would take her through an entire year in Kingsford. And even if she cut down on her nights at the bar, she'd still be making more than she was in New York, with a better schedule on top of it.

And she'd get to keep seeing Bianca. Which was both as thrilling as it was terrifying. Did Bianca want more from her? She hadn't asked Maeve when she was leaving again, seemingly content to let their time play out together. It was something Maeve had been trying not to think about, and it felt like a lot of pressure to put on such a fledgling relationship.

It's not like she'd only be staying because of Bianca. She had a whole list now. Except, she'd be lying to herself if she said Bianca wasn't at the top of it. And that in itself was a whole other problem she'd been trying not to think about the past few weeks.

May as well add one more thing to her growing list. "Can I have a little time to think about it? This would be a bigger commitment than my work with Sawyer."

Quinn nodded. "Sure thing. I'm reaching out early. Like I said, there's work now, but the bulk of it won't start for another few months. Let me know when you make a decision," she said, already walking toward the front door.

Maeve nodded dumbly at Quinn's retreating form. Sure.

She'd just make a decision. Like that wasn't going to have all kinds of consequences for her life—and her heart.

* * *

It was the last Monday in January, and Bianca could barely contain her surprise when Maeve had suggested they spend the night somewhere other than the warmth of Bianca's house.

Which is how she found herself at the Kingsford bowling alley.

She and Maeve were seated at one of the tables above the lanes, watching Jonny, her dad, and Patrick Murphy, along with the rest of their team, huddled together before their game started.

She shot a glance in Maeve's direction, who looked unfairly good in a distressed pair of jeans and a tank top layered with a flannel. Usually, that clothing would already be on Bianca's floor.

But this was nice too, getting to spend time around Kingsford with Maeve, even if it wasn't their normal routine. When Maeve had asked, she had no false expectations that this was a date. Bianca knew Maeve and her dad were working to mend their relationship, and this was a sweet attempt from Maeve to make sure she knew what was going on in her dad's life and share something that was important to him.

Conversely, Bianca wondered if Patrick Murphy knew what was going on in his daughter's life? Maeve wasn't her girlfriend though, and she hadn't expected her to be sharing news of their hookups across town.

"Jonny is never going to let me hear the end of this," Bianca said with mock exasperation, trying to quiet the discomfort in her brain.

Maeve took a sip of her beer and turned her body inward toward Bianca, their knees brushing lightly. "Why?"

"Because I never come to watch him bowl, in spite of his insistence."

"But you are watching him bowl," Maeve said as she gestured out toward the lane.

Bianca dropped her voice lower. "We both know that's not why I'm here."

She liked the little flush of color that bloomed across Maeve's cheeks. "I'm glad you decided to come. I would have come over after but this is... nice."

It was difficult not to reach under the table and grab Maeve's hand. Their touches had grown so much easier inside of Bianca's house, and treating her like any other person was becoming increasingly difficult. On Friday night at the bar, she'd accidentally grabbed Maeve's ass as she'd walked by, only realizing where they were when Maeve's drink shaker clattered on the bar.

Compartmentalizing her worlds was growing increasingly more difficult. They weren't intentionally being secretive, but it was the dead of winter and with only a few weeknights to spend together, events in public were limited.

Bianca groaned when she saw Jonny sauntering toward them. "Well, well well, look what the cat dragged in."

"Hi, Jonny," Maeve said, surprisingly congenial. Bianca gave her a confused side-eye but didn't mention it. She wasn't going to look a gift horse in the mouth.

"Prying yourself away from Monday movie night," he said, making air quotes. "I wondered what it would take to drag you out of the house."

"Well, I'm here." Bianca hoped the warning in her voice abated him, but she never knew where her best friend was concerned.

They still managed dinner once a week, and even if Maeve was a huge part of her life, she'd been resistant to go into all the details with him. Picking apart her feelings would only lead to more confusion.

Jonny gave them both a charming smile. "Maeve, you're looking well."

"Must be all the clean country air," she said drily.

"You seem to be enjoying it. I'm surprised you're still in town."

She felt Maeve's leg tighten next to hers, and she shot daggers at Jonny, knowing they'd be having a conversation about this later. For as frustrated as she was with him for opening the box of things that were not spoken about, it was a question that she'd thought about more than a few times the last few weeks.

"Are you requesting an updated itinerary as my plans evolve or...?"

He shrugged his shoulders, like the answer didn't matter too much either way. "Just curious. Well, looks like I'm up," he said, shooting them one last smile before sauntering back to his lane.

"I didn't put him up to that."

Maeve looked at her with bright blue eyes, her forehead scrunched in confusion. "I didn't think you did."

"I just..." Bianca stalled, looking out toward the lanes. "I know we haven't really talked about things, so I didn't want you to think this was some juvenile attempt to extract information."

Leaning closer, Maeve ghosted her fingertips across Bianca's jean-clad thigh. "You're usually pretty vocal. I don't doubt that if you want something, you'll tell me."

In a lot of situations, yes. But when it came to telling Maeve that Bianca wanted *her*, the words got stuck in her throat.

"You know me," she flirted back, shooting Maeve a toothy smile and willing her erratic heartbeat to slow down.

Everything about her, including her words, felt a little stuck right now, and she didn't know what she was going to do about it.

* * *

By Thursday, Maeve couldn't hold it in anymore. She had to say something to someone. Shirley, whether her gym buddy liked it or not, had become that lucky person.

"What if I stay?"

Shirley finished her last three reps and eased the machine into its rest position. "Stay in Kingsford?"

"Yes."

"Well, I think that all depends on why you're staying. A sense of obligation isn't going to get you very far in terms of happiness."

Maeve shook her head. "It's not that."

She watched Shirley as Shirley watched her, a curious smile on the other woman's face. "Well, then what is it?"

Maeve groaned. She'd started this, but expressing her feelings was still hard. "I like it here."

"What do you like about it?"

"I like my routine. I like the projects I'm working on. I like our time at the gym."

Shirley nodded slowly. "Anything else?"

Maeve let out an indignant huff. "You know there is."

She'd made the mistake of talking to Shirley more about Bianca a few weeks ago. The Saturday morning after Bianca had fucked Maeve to within an inch of her senses at the bar, she'd woken up in Bianca's bed, sleeping peacefully as the little spoon with their legs tangled up together.

Cuffing Season

It had been a lot to process, mostly because of how much Maeve liked it, spending the whole night together and waking up with her in the morning. And how much she'd wanted to keep doing it.

The whole thing had been terrifyingly normal. Bianca had placed light, lingering kisses on Maeve's shoulder before sliding out of bed to make coffee. Then, they'd laid around in their pajamas, Maeve doing a crossword puzzle she'd found on the coffee table and Bianca engaging in one of her favorite activities, looking at pets up for adoption at the local shelter.

Domesticity had never been something Maeve had craved, but without having some big conversation about it, she'd started sleeping over on nights they hooked up. She wondered how long they could keep doing this without putting a name to it.

It was easy, being with Bianca, but it didn't feel at all casual in spite of their initial agreement. Maybe it would—or could—have been, except for the feelings.

"Have you told her you're thinking about staying?" Shirley finally asked after the prolonged silence between them.

"No."

"Well, maybe that's a good place to start. I know you think this town is tiny, but it's big enough for the both of you. And I'm sure she won't assume that she's the only reason you're staying."

But what if she is, when compared to all the others?

"Well, I've got a card game later," Shirley said as she stood up from the machine. "I can't tell you what to do, but I can tell you that most people like feeling like they matter." She gave Maeve a pointed look and said, "It's not something that causes the average-well adjusted person to go running for the hills."

"And we both know which type of person you think I am."

"Doesn't mean you can't have what you want. Just means

you need to do the chasing so that you're still running, but it's toward something."

The possibility caused a flutter of anticipation in her stomach. Maeve had never been the type of woman to think she could have it all. She'd settled for trying to have one thing—a successful career—and even that wasn't going according to plan.

Getting family, job, friends, and the woman who seemed a little too good to be true was—well, it hadn't been her experience in life so far.

But Bianca had already shown her a lot of things she hadn't thought possible. It felt good to hope that maybe they could be one of them.

Chapter Twenty

When Maeve let herself in on Monday night, as had become the standard for their visits, Bianca knew she looked like a wreck. It wasn't the joggers or ratty sweatshirt. Or her ponytail that wasn't stylishly messy—just actually sloppy as she'd thrown her hair up when she'd gotten home from work.

"Are you crying?" Maeve asked after she dropped her overnight bag at the entry—another thing that had started happening, even if Bianca couldn't pinpoint exactly when.

She blew her nose and plucked another tissue from the holder to wipe a tear that had fallen. "I'm usually better than this. I just had a really hard day at work," Bianca said, trying to get the words out but finding it difficult with her breath catching.

Maeve was next to her in a second. She hunched down in front of Bianca and cupped her jaw. "What's wrong? What happened? Are you okay?"

Hands skimming along her chin and cheeks, she leaned into the comfort of the touch. "I'm sorry I'm such a wreck. I should have told you before you came over. I thought I'd be able to stop crying."

When she felt Maeve's fingers pull her chin up, their eyes met. "I'm so sorry about whatever happened. Do you want to talk about it? Can I get you anything?"

She felt more than she saw Maeve stand up. A second later, Maeve was next to her on the sofa, pulling Bianca into her and running her fingers soothingly along Bianca's temple.

All that did was make Bianca cry harder, finally letting the tears she'd been trying to hold in fall. It had been a long time since she'd gotten so emotional about something at work, but she'd felt like her heart had truly broken today. Every time she thought about it, the tears began flowing, followed by hiccups when she tried to hold in her exhales.

"It's okay, baby." Maeve held her tighter, sliding down so Bianca's weight could rest on her. She didn't stop her gentle caresses, strong arms encircling Bianca while she cried herself out.

Her eyes were red and raw when she finally stopped. Sitting up seemed insurmountable, but she needed to blow her nose.

"I cried all over your shirt," Bianca noticed when she managed to pull her body almost upright.

Maeve leaned forward and grabbed Bianca a tissue. "It doesn't matter."

Maeve here, doing and saying all the right things was both comforting and confusing. She'd finally calmed down, but it was replaced with an emptiness, like she was already experiencing what it would feel like when this comfort was gone.

"Do you want to talk about it?" Maeve asked after Bianca blew her nose for the dozenth time tonight.

She leaned her side against the sofa cushions and tucked her feet underneath her. "I mean... it was just a sad day."

Cuffing Season

"But you're okay?" The concern radiating from Maeve was palpable as she found Bianca's hand and interlaced their fingers.

"I'm okay. It was just one of those freak things. A car saw something on the side of the road and stopped. It was a mother and three puppies. The mom had already been hit by a car and the puppies were cuddled into her trying to stay warm. The driver brought all of them in, but the mom and two of the puppies didn't make it." As she said the words, she felt the tears start to fall again, but she couldn't stop them.

"Oh god, Bianca. I'm so sorry. Come here." Maeve pulled her into a surprisingly soft hug given how tightly she was holding Bianca in her arms.

For a moment, all of Bianca's sadness was washed away—so was the emptiness—and she felt the full strength of what Maeve in her life, through the good and the bad, could mean. Comfort and solace and passion and support.

It was everything she wanted, and as she nuzzled herself into Maeve's neck, Bianca wondered if she could be the one to have it with.

What did Maeve want? That was the real question, and one until this moment, she'd been too afraid to ask.

She let out a long exhale and placed a light kiss against Maeve's collarbone. When she sat up, she met Maeve's concerned stare. It was unsurprising that crying for the last thirty minutes had made Maeve more than a little worried for her stability.

"Feel any better?" Maeve asked softly, stroking her fingers down Bianca's arm. "I'm so sorry that happened. So, so sorry."

"Did you decide when you're leaving yet?"

The worry in Maeve's eyes shifted into something inscrutable.

Bianca let the silence linger, not realizing until this moment how much she needed an answer. Because doing what they were doing was one thing, but wondering every time she saw Maeve if today would be the moment she told her she'd picked a definitive departure date—when she finally had enough of the town that Bianca loved—wasn't something she could handle anymore.

Maeve finally nodded, like she was gearing herself up to speak. "I don't really know. Things in Kingsford with my dad and the bar and picking up work are going surprisingly well. I guess I'm kind of just seeing how things play out."

"Oh," Bianca said, a wave of elation hitting her before one of despair followed after. Maeve liked it here, but didn't like what they were doing enough to change the expectations of their relationship. Not enough to bring it up without Bianca's prompting. The idea of that hurt worse than Maeve actually leaving.

"It's not really something I've officially decided yet, or something I was intentionally keeping from you." Maeve's face looked sincere, but her voice wavered when she spoke, like there was more to it.

"Yeah, no. That makes sense." Bianca nodded, feeling more than a little bit like an idiot. Suddenly, Maeve's comfort felt like an anchor, dragging her below the surface and making it hard to breathe. She wiped a rogue tear from her cheek and squeezed Maeve's hand before disentangling their fingers. When she stood up, she glanced at the clock on the wall before pulling her eyes back to Maeve. "I'm not going to be very good company tonight. Do you mind if we catch up later?"

Maeve scrambled to a standing position and fidgeted with the silver ring she wore on her right hand. "Are you okay? I don't feel right leaving you alone right now."

Was she okay? Not really, but she didn't want Maeve to see that. She'd already fallen apart once tonight. Twice seemed a little excessive, even for her. "Honestly, I'm just going to head to bed. Thank you for sitting with me. It helped a lot."

Taking a small step forward, Maeve placed her hand on Bianca's forearm. It felt good, the warmth and softness and comfort that radiated from Maeve's touch. But it wasn't enough anymore.

"I'm happy to hang out with you. I'm not angling to stay here just to get in your bed."

Bianca dropped her arm down to her side, breaking the contact with Maeve. It was the only way she could make herself send her away. "I know. I'd just rather be alone. Sorry to have you come over here and deal with me blubbering, only to head back home."

Maeve didn't protest again, but she also didn't call Bianca's reticence out. It felt like they were both reluctant to disrupt the status quo.

"You'll text me if you need anything?" Maeve asked when she picked up her bag next to the entryway.

Bianca followed her to the door. "Absolutely, but I'll probably be asleep within the hour. Crying always makes me tired."

She faltered when Maeve's hand came up to cup her jaw gently before pulling her into a soft, sweet kiss. "I'm sorry you had a rough day. Please let me know if I can do anything to make it better."

Love me? Be with me? Not be afraid to put a name to this thing between us? "Thanks, I will."

Thirty seconds later, Bianca was alone in her house, wondering how the worst day she'd had in a long time had managed to get worse.

* * *

Maeve hadn't slept well last night, but she lugged herself out of bed the next morning to meet Shirley at the gym. She'd sent Bianca a text after getting home, met with a thumbs up and nothing more.

At least she'd gotten that. Bianca, for whatever reason, had basically given her the brush off. Grief did strange things to people. When her mom had died, she'd thrown herself into working at the bar, but when she'd come home, every free moment was spent in her room alone to process her sadness.

The problem was, it's not what she'd expected from Bianca. Leaning into Maeve's offer of comfort was what she'd expected, and her lack of sleep came from wondering if they were starting to get close to a conversation that was long overdue. Maybe Bianca was tired of Maeve. Or now that she'd realized she was staying, figured it was better to cut ties, since she couldn't see herself with Maeve long-term.

That put a terrifying wrench in the plans Maeve had finally started dreaming were possible.

It's not like she didn't realize having both sides of the conversation wasn't productive, but last night hadn't felt right, when Bianca was already dealing with a stressful situation.

She'd talk to her tonight, that is, if they were still going to see one another.

After shoveling down a protein bar, she grabbed her gym bag and headed out. There was another conversation she needed to have, and running into her dad as he was grabbing the mail at the end of their driveway presented the perfect opportunity.

He waved the newspaper in her direction, nonplussed by the cold. "Hey, Maeve."

She tightened her hand around the strap of her gym bag. "Got a minute?"

"Anything for you. What's up?"

She saw the same dimple appear in her dad's cheek that she had, realizing she hadn't seen it since being back until this moment. It felt a little bit like a north star, showing her that she was making the right decision.

Mirroring his smile, she didn't waste any time given that her hands were already going numb from the cold. "I was thinking about staying."

"Staying?" The word rolled off his tongue like he didn't quite understand. To be fair, she was as surprised as he was.

She squinted into the morning sun. "For a while at least. I can get my own place if you'd prefer but... I don't know, it seems like we have a good little thing going here. Are you open to continuing on as roomies?"

Expecting an answer, she let out a puff of air when her dad enveloped her in a crushing hug. His arm wrapped around the back of her head, and she felt the light scruff of his beard against her cheek. "Always. For as long as you're happy here, you always have a home with me."

"Thanks, Dad. I love you." Her voice was thick with emotion, and she realized she was fighting tears threatening to spill over.

Finally, he let her go from the hug, but he still kept a hand loosely wrapped around her jacket-clad bicep, the other wiping his eye. "I love you, too," she said, giving her arm one last squeeze before dropping his hand. "Chili tonight?"

She laughed at the normalcy of it all, and how much she didn't mind it one bit. "I don't think I'll be around tonight."

"Oh right. You're usually at Bianca's tonight."

Her brows drew upward. She'd never told him that. "Um... yeah. How'd you know that?"

He shrugged and grinned. "Small town. Plus, I have eyes."

All the times the three of them had been together over the last few months, she'd been doing anything but look at him to keep the awkwardness of their interactions at bay. She hadn't thought about what he'd been seeing instead.

Maeve cleared her throat, like she was a teenager being caught. "It's really not..." She stopped herself. Because it was a big deal. She wanted it to be a big deal. "Yes. I've been with Bianca."

"And you like her?"

Her face would betray any lies she told, so there was no point. "Very much."

"Does she like you?"

Trickier topic after last night. "Seems like some days more than others."

Her dad looked at his steel-toed boots and shuffled his feet before meeting her eyes. They really were a pair. "I know you're an adult and probably way beyond the dispensing of fatherly advice, but you and I, we aren't the best at sharing our emotions. So, all I'm saying is that if you care, you need to tell her. Be really clear about it. I should have told your mom more." His voice caught then, blue eyes shiny with tears close to falling.

"She knew, dad. Don't doubt that."

"Either way, I should tell you more. I *should have told* you more. I love you, and I'm so proud of you. Whatever you do. Wherever you go. Whoever you're with. Nothing will change that, okay?"

The tears that had been prickling behind her eyes started to fall, spurred on by her dad's same blue eyes looking at her, now full of tears too.

She wiped them away and sniffled. "Well, shit," she said with a choked laugh. "I need to meet my friend, Shirley, at the gym. And if I don't get in the car soon, I'm going to lose a couple of fingers."

"One last thing."

Maeve nodded and rubbed her hands together.

"I was going to see if Pete wanted to take on some extra shifts or if you wanted me to hire someone else. Not to take your place, but if you wanted to work fewer hours to have time to focus on photography or just have a little more time to relax."

"That's..." Exactly what she would have done. Doing something instead of saying something. "That's really sweet, dad. How about tomorrow night we look everything over and come up with a plan?"

"Sounds good."

When Maeve got in her car, she texted Shirley that she'd be late. She needed at least a few minutes to let her appendages warm up, and a few more for good measure to come down from whatever had just happened.

And once she was warm enough to think again, she needed to figure out how to tell Bianca exactly how she felt about her. She only hoped that Bianca felt the same way too.

* * *

On Thursday night, Bianca met Jonny at Zorba's to grab dinner. All of her other suggestions had been vetoed, and she was more than a little annoyed to be here.

Which he could clearly tell when he said, tactful as always, "What stick is stuck up your ass tonight?"

Bianca folded her arms across her chest. "I just think Vito's would have been better."

"Bullshit. Vito's hasn't been good since the son took over and started skimping on the toppings." He wasn't wrong, but she wasn't going to admit that.

She tried to slip her next comment casually into their conversation. "On the off-chance you run into Maeve, you and I had dinner on Tuesday, too."

Jonny lifted a perfectly sculpted brow. "Did we now?"

"Yes, we did. Don't make it a thing." Bianca busied herself dipping a piece of pita into their shared hummus.

"Why are you avoiding Maeve? Trouble in paradise?"

"I'm not." She shoved a too-big bite into her mouth to give her a few seconds of silence. At least, she was silent. Jonny had other ideas.

"You're usually direct. I've never had to run interference for you before. That's my thing." He sighed dramatically. "I'm starting to feel a little bit lost in this friendship."

Waving him off, Bianca pretended to focus on her menu. "The tilapia salad looks good."

"Bianca. Look at me."

She could count on one hand the number of times in her life she'd felt this adrift—on edge in a way that was bleeding into her entire existence.

"What?" she finally asked, meeting Jonny's stare.

"What's going on with you? Are you okay?"

"Why does everyone keep asking me that?" The words came out louder than she expected, Jonny's eyes going wide.

"Is this about what happened at work on Monday? Or is this about Maeve? Something else?"

She'd told Jonny about the puppies and mom on Tuesday morning, when she'd been able to go into the office and see that the last living puppy was still hanging in there. Dr. Anderson had taken the puppy who'd survived home with her for the last three nights to make sure she got the proper care, and by today, they were confident she'd make it.

"I'm still heartbroken about what happened to those dogs, but this is mostly about Maeve."

"Unburden yourself." Jonny reached his hands across the table, making grabby motions.

Bianca chewed at the inside of her lip. She felt juvenile that it had come to this. "Well, on Monday night, she came over to hang out."

Jonny nodded. "If that's what the kids are calling it."

"Do you want me to tell you or not?"

He pretended to zip his lips.

"Good. So, she was like... absolutely perfect," Bianca said, unable to stop the wistfulness in her voice. "So sweet and supportive and just there for me. It felt like one of those moments when everything could change."

"And did it? Change I mean," Jonny clarified.

"Suddenly, waiting for the other shoe to drop where she tells me she's leaving felt impossible, so I asked her."

"There's the directness I love."

Bianca shook her head. "She was... vague."

Jonny swirled his glass of wine. "Elaborate."

It took all of Bianca's energy not to drop her head into her hands and sulk. Instead, she took a quick sip of wine and rolled her shoulders. "She told me things with her dad and the bar were going well and that she wanted to 'see how things played out,'" Bianca said, adding air quotes during the last part.

Jonny regarded her with an inscrutable look. "That doesn't sound bad. Why are we mad?"

"We're not mad. We're just accepting that maybe this thing between me and Maeve has run its course."

"Aww, damn. I was finally starting to warm up to her."

Bianca rolled her eyes. "No you weren't."

"Well, I was warming up to the idea of warming up to her. I feel like that counts." Bianca didn't pull away when he reached across the table and enveloped her hand. "All I know is that you've been happier these last few months, and I don't think it's just because you're getting laid regularly."

"Classy, Jonny," she said, though her smile betrayed her.

"It just sounds like there's a little bit of self-sabotage going on here." She glared at him and tried to pull her hand away, but he held on. "You need to get out of your own way. Woman up. Have a real conversation. Figure out where things stand."

When Jonny let go of her hand, she slumped back in her chair. "I really like her. It would kill me if she doesn't feel the same way."

"From where I sit, you're the problem here. She was there for you Monday. She spends all her free time with you. She's staying in town. Do you need her to write out her intentions in Christmas lights in the town square?"

"Christmas is over."

"Fine," he scoffed. "Heart-shaped candy, then. Don't get distracted by the example. It was for illustrative purposes only."

Bianca's voice grew quiet. "I just haven't felt this way in a really long time. I'm afraid of what happens if it goes wrong."

"But think of what could happen if it goes right."

"You're really annoying when you're the positive one."

Jonny let out a loud laugh. "Then get your shit together so that I don't have to be anymore!"

She'd see Maeve tomorrow night, whether or not she was ready for their conversation. Hopefully, she could find the courage to tell her how she felt by then.

Chapter Twenty-One

Maeve didn't stop moving until they shut down the bar. It was great news for her dad and the future of Murph's, but working five nights a week was starting to take a toll on her.

She'd talked with her dad on Tuesday, when she'd unexpectedly found herself at home, and together, they'd figured out what the next few months could look like. Maeve would still work three nights a week, but they'd hire someone new and while she trained them up, she'd formally be implementing the bar program that already de facto existed.

Bianca wouldn't need to cover on Fridays unless she wanted to anymore, and even though the idea of not seeing her at Murph's caused a little pang in her chest, she hoped it would leave more time for them to spend together outside of work.

Her job with Sawyer had wrapped up earlier today, but there were still five to ten hours a week photographing new inventory or items ship-ready for insurance purposes if she wanted them. And Quinn, who was honestly a little intimidating with how organized she was, had already sent Maeve a preliminary proposal for their work together.

The real estate photography would start slowly, mostly photos of the office Quinn had just completed renovations on, in what used to be the original Kent Antiques. And, as she'd learned last week, conveniently right in front of where Sawyer and Quinn lived.

She felt like everything was finally falling into place.

Except one thing...

Bianca, maybe to avoid her, had taken over the bulk of the cleaning duties tonight, situated safely across from Maeve as she cleaned the tables, swept the bar, and flipped the chairs.

All Maeve had wanted to do tonight when Bianca had walked in was rush over to her and throw her arms around her. But, for a multitude of reasons, she hadn't.

Now, there were no customers to help. No buffer between them except a shared unwillingness to put their hearts on the line.

"Bianca?" Maeve said to get her attention, surprised at the softness in her voice. Maeve had been hard edges for as long as she could remember, except when it came to anything involving Bianca Rossi.

"Busy night tonight." Bianca kept sweeping, refusing to meet her eye.

Maeve walked around the bar and plucked the broom from Bianca's hands before leaning it against a booth. "You already did that spot."

When Bianca's eyes shifted upward to meet her stare, she saw the same fear she felt in her own reflecting back at her. They both knew what this was, and she wasn't going to be afraid to say it any more.

"Can we talk?"

Maeve had never seen Bianca this nervous. It would have been cute, if she wasn't so on edge too.

Bianca gulped audibly. "Yes. We probably should."

Instinctively, Maeve grabbed one of Bianca's hands and interlaced their fingers. She didn't know if it would hurt or help the conversation, but it felt like the right thing to do. "First, I wanted to talk about Monday."

Tension radiated from Bianca's tall frame, but Maeve didn't back away. "Thanks again for being there for me. It meant a lot."

Maeve nodded. "I'm glad. But I feel like after I told you I was staying in town, the tone of the night kinda changed. Did you notice that?"

"I just..." Bianca let out a heavy sigh, amplified by the silence in the room. "You didn't really give me any details. You didn't bring *us* up. If you're staying, and relationships aren't your thing, I didn't want you to think that I expected anything from you."

Maeve's heart jackhammered in her chest. "I want you to expect things from me."

"You didn't make it seem like that Monday night."

"Well, I was talking to my dad..."

Bianca cut her off, tone strangled when she asked, "You talked to your dad about us?"

"He knew already," Maeve said with a shrug. That wasn't a problem as far as she was concerned, since there was no one she was more proud to be seen with than Bianca.

"God, that must be why my dad keeps saying you guys should come over for dinner. I feel like the Kingsford men's bowling league could give any gossip circle a run for its money."

Maeve smiled and let the moment of normalcy wash over them before she ran her free hand through her tousled hair. She must have already done it a hundred times tonight in her anxiousness. "The thing is, when we talked on Monday, I didn't want *you* to feel pressured." She squeezed Bianca's fingers and met green eyes that she'd fallen hopelessly in love with over the last few months. She knew that for sure now. "I want to be with you. I want us to go on dates and watch ridiculously cheesy movies together. I want all the things that a year ago, I'd have made fun of other people for doing."

Bianca let out a little snort-laugh, but her shoulders were still tight, like she was waiting for the but to come. "That is a very you thing to say."

"I came back here under probably the worst circumstances I could imagine."

Bianca frowned, and she inched closer as she squeezed Maeve's hand back. "I know. I'm so sorry that happened."

"It was awful, and I was awful. I already wasn't exactly the most positive person, but I just felt so... broken."

It was so gentle, the way Bianca lifted her hand up to cup Maeve's jaw, running her fingers over Maeve's bottom lip. "You're not broken."

"I don't think you realize everything you've already done for me," Maeve said seriously. "I don't even think that I realized truly how much until I saw you crying on Monday. At that moment, I couldn't imagine not being there for you when you needed someone. I *wanted* to be that person for you, to take away any amount of your pain that I could."

She could hear traces of wariness in Bianca's voice, like she still didn't believe it even as she asked, "So, you want to do this? You want us to do this?"

"I want to be the one who kills the spiders for you." And Maeve waited, waited until Bianca's lips tipped upward into a radiant smile before leaning forward and ghosting their mouths together in a kiss that was so sweet it could have been the ending to one of the many movies she'd secretly grown to love.

"Come home with me tonight?" Bianca asked between kisses that were growing more frenzied by the second. Her hand had found its way into Maeve's hair, the question thrown in between nipping at Maeve's bottom lip and then easing her tongue inside, licking into Maeve's mouth with an intensity that took her breath away.

Maeve's heart fluttered when she felt Bianca's hand squeeze her hip before warm fingertips skimmed along her stomach. And that shifted attention from the flutter in her heart to the ache in her center, growing more persistent as Bianca's tongue did things that should probably be illegal.

"Yes," Maeve said when she had enough control to pull her mouth away, knowing her future self would be happier once they got back to Bianca's house. She gave her one last kiss, which took all of her resolve not to deepen, before she shifted back and looked into Bianca's bright eyes. "I don't want to be anywhere else."

* * *

"Do you think I can't keep my hands to myself?" Bianca asked as Maeve fastened the strap on the second handcuff to her headboard.

Maeve didn't answer immediately, and instead, she ran her finger up and down Bianca's forearm, her eyes following the same pattern of her movements.

They'd gotten back to Bianca's house fifteen minutes ago. As a direct consequence of Bianca's inability to keep her hands to herself, which only one of them saw as a problem, she found herself complying to Maeve's request to 'show Bianca' exactly how she felt about her.

"Can you?" Maeve's eyes drew up to meet hers, and Bianca smirked at the slightly wide, slightly dazed look on them. Glad to know she wasn't the only one feeling a bit out of sorts, although she had very little recourse if her words didn't work.

"I don't know," Bianca admitted, drawing in a sharp breath when Maeve dragged a finger down Bianca's chest. The sensation ricocheted through her body, and she heard a light, low chuckle escape Maeve's lips. It was sweet and soft and for as frustrated as she was that Maeve was making her wait, the sound filled her like a balloon as her love and want and desire threatened to push out through her body from every pore.

Bianca watched the muscles in Maeve's neck flex, could see her abs clenched tightly as she continued her soft, exploratory touches along Bianca's exposed skin. At this rate, it wouldn't take much to push her over the edge. Between Maeve's admission in the bar and the skilled fingers plucking at her nipple, she'd already clenched her thighs to find some sort of relief from the mounting pressure.

Maeve shifted her legs off Bianca and sat next to her on the bed near her knees. Her fingertips skimmed upward across Bianca's thighs, drawing another moan from her lips, the muscles of her legs hard and tense under Maeve's hands.

When Maeve finally reached the band of her underwear, she took in another sharp breath.

"Baby, please," Bianca said, her voice strangled with the force of Maeve's teasing. All she was right now was a mass of vibrating molecules that felt on the verge of combustion.

Maeve had found the words earlier, and now, she was showing her with touches and caresses and soft sighs that made Bianca wonder how quickly she'd come undone.

When Maeve plucked at the band of fabric on her underwear, soft against Bianca's skin, her body radiated heat that wanted to push through the garment and engulf the entire room. And then, she hooked her fingers into the band and pulled, Bianca immediately shifting upward to comply with the request.

"Seems like you're starting to come around," Maeve said as she worked the underwear down Bianca's knees.

Bianca let out a sound between a groan and a sob when Maeve's fingertips played down the inside of her thigh. "You're killing me."

"Let me take care of you." It wasn't a command. It was a request, Maeve's voice full and throaty, her lips parted and her cheeks flushed as she took Bianca in.

Bianca nodded, and Maeve shifted her legs apart so that she could settle astride them. Maeve started at Bianca's ankles, running her fingers up the skin of her shins, Bianca both tensing and melting into the touch simultaneously. When Maeve got to her knees, she stilled her hands and pushed downward, Bianca's feet pressing and flexing into the bed in response.

It felt excruciatingly good when Maeve leaned forward to run her palms down Bianca's thighs, shifting her hands slowly toward where her legs met her hips. Bianca's head shifted back, her eyes lidded, her breathing slow. It was almost tantric, how her body worked to find a sense of balance, a calm amidst the chaos that Maeve's skilled hands were wreaking across every inch of skin they touched.

"I hope you know how much I want this. Us," Maeve said as her fingers ghosted across Bianca's center.

"I do," Bianca pushed out between increasingly difficult breaths. And now that she could let herself feel it fully, her pleasure was magnified to a point of almost incomprehension.

"And I want to kiss you," Maeve said as she skimmed her fingers across the skin just below Bianca's belly button, tracing lazy patterns that made Bianca feel like she was going to come apart.

Bianca managed a soft, ragged laugh, her stomach pushing back against Maeve's fingertips. "All I'm managing to do right now is breathe, so yes, let's make that a challenge, too," Bianca managed to say, her words choppy.

"No, not here," Maeve said as she pushed forward and ran her fingers across Bianca's trembling lips before cupping her jaw and making soothing circles with her fingers.

Bianca's brow furrowed as she panted lightly against Maeve's finger. Understanding anything was almost impossible right now. "Wh-" Her eyes popped open wide, and she rolled her hips up toward Maeve above her. "You're trying to kill me."

Maeve licked her lips in response. "I want to taste you."

"Yes," Bianca said as her eyes flitted closed again, as her body tensed in preparation for what was about to happen next. "Please."

Maeve scooted back on the bed and dropped her head down, almost flush with Bianca's center. Bianca drew in a breath, her focus spinning out with the soft, warm exhales of Maeve's breaths against her clit.

And then, Maeve slipped her hands around Bianca's thighs to brace them, her legs already slightly shaky although she hadn't even been touched yet.

Maeve moved forward and kissed Bianca's skin before slipping her tongue out and licking gently into Bianca's center. Her legs spasmed with the touch, and she let the hot pleasure sprawl across her body.

"Baby," Bianca panted from the top of the bed, her head thrown back as her chest rose and fell as Maeve continued to lick slowly.

Maeve flattened her tongue against Bianca and gave a long, purposeful stroke up her center, stopping just short of her clit. Bianca moaned in response and opened her eyes to stare down at Maeve. Impossibly deep blue eyes met her own. She couldn't take her eyes off of Maeve, both of them watching one another as Maeve licked into her.

"I like when you watch me," Maeve said before wrapping her lips around Bianca's clit, the jolt of pleasure making her arch off the bed.

"Oh my god," Bianca said as she threw her arm against her forehead. "That's a good thing because I really, really like watching you. Your tongue feels so good. I don't know how much longer I can last."

Maeve bit her lip as she licked her tongue broadly against Bianca's center and ran her fingers along the plane of her stomach. "Do you want to come?"

"Yes," Bianca breathed. "But I don't want to be tied up for it. I want to touch you." She stilled and looked back down at Maeve. "I *need* to be able to touch you."

"Is that so?" Maeve asked as she pushed her fingers harder against Bianca's stomach and dragged them lower.

Bianca nodded and pulled against the cuffs as she bit her lip. "Please. I can't imagine not feeling you right now. You've already got me, Maeve. Let me touch you."

Without speaking, Maeve began to unfasten the cuffs. As soon as they dropped, Bianca darted her arm forward and ran her hand down Maeve's side, pushing hungrily into the skin.

"Baby, please." Bianca had already snaked her arm between them, her other hand fastened to Maeve's hip as she tried to grind their bodies together, rolling her hips upward in search of friction.

She saw white when Maeve's hand slipped downward and circled her clit purposefully, fingers matching the same tempo as Maeve's tongue when it found her mouth, capturing her lips in a kiss that muffled the moan as she fell over the edge.

Their bodies wrapped around one another, connected at every point possible as Bianca came down from her orgasm was unlike anything she'd ever experienced before.

Probably because she was hopelessly in love with a person

who she was pretty sure loved her back. It made all the difference, when Maeve dropped the weight from her forearm to lay astride Bianca, all she wanted to do was wrap Maeve up in her arms and place kisses along every inch of skin within reach.

So she did.

When her breathing finally evened out, she continued to trace shapes along Maeve's back, working up the strength to return the favor as soon as she could feel her legs again.

"I guess we officially failed at cuffing season," Bianca said absently, her fingers wandering over to Maeve's ribcage.

Maeve nuzzled into her shoulder and placed a light kiss against her collarbone before sighing contently. "I'm not really sure how I thought I could spend all this time with you and not fall in love."

Bianca's heart skipped a beat, her fingers stilling. "You love me?"

Maeve nodded, and when Bianca shifted her focus down, the little dimple she loved so much was on display, an embarrassed smile on Maeve's face. "I'm trying to get better at talking about my feelings, but yes. I love you. Didn't really seem helpful to keep it inside. It's okay if you're not there yet or—"

Bianca cut her off at the same time she shifted quickly to roll Maeve on her back, easily slotting their bodies together with Bianca on top. "Don't be stupid. Of course I love you. I've been in agony this last week worrying about how you felt and whether I was all alone in this."

"Not alone. Never," Maeve said as she wrapped her arms around Bianca and pulled her down for a kiss that was the start of the first moment of the rest of her life.

Epilogue

September, 2022

Maeve leaned into Bianca and placed a light kiss on her temple. "This wedding is insane."

Understatement of the year. Quinn and Sawyer's wedding, though small in number of guests, looked like something out of a bridal magazine. She'd met the wedding planners, Lily and Bennett, a few times, but none of the conversations she'd heard had prepared her for the charm infused in every thoughtful touch at the winery where the wedding was being held, about thirty minutes outside of Kingsford.

But what else should Bianca expect of Kingsford's newest power couple?

Sawyer's antiques business had taken off over the last year, boosted by her online presence, and she was now getting requests from all over the world. The Victorian location, where Bianca had stopped by last week to drop off lunch for Maeve, was practically bursting with inventory that would be gone in a matter of weeks.

Quinn's real estate company, buoyed by the interest from New Yorkers as well as her dogged tenacity, had been busy non-stop through the summer and fall. The only time she ever saw Quinn without her phone was today, when she'd handed it to Maeve and told her not to give it back under any circumstances.

"I've gotta get up there," Maeve said when she saw the wedding planner give the five-minute call that the ceremony was about to start.

A year ago, if you'd have told Bianca that Maeve would be standing up as a person-of-honor at Quinn and Sawyer's wedding, she'd have laughed. But as she watched her girlfriend stroll up to the altar, dressed in a dapper, fitted navy suit, it made perfect sense now. She loved how close to one another the two previously commitment-phobic blondes had grown. Quinn's sister, Kelly, was standing up with Sawyer, already wiping away tears.

From her spot, Maeve brushed a piece of hair out of her face and gave Bianca a dorky thumbs up and a bashful smile. She'd been almost embarrassed when she'd told Bianca that Quinn had asked, like she couldn't quite believe that anyone would think so highly of her to put her in their wedding party. If only Maeve knew how much the people of Kingsford loved her, and how she'd earned it just by showing up and *doing*, and making herself a person they could depend on.

Bianca also had a job at the wedding, so she stepped away from where she was gawking at her girlfriend and headed to the end of the aisle to meet Trevor Warren, Kelly's husband, and their daughters. Luna and Ella were happily entertained, playing with Bianca's now one-year-old pup, Gemelli Rossi— Gem for short. What was she going to do? Not name the dog

Maeve had suggested Bianca adopt after both of their favorite pasta noodle?

Bianca would guide Gem down the aisle as the official ring bearer, which they'd been practicing for weeks together.

It had been Maeve who'd suggested looking into whether the dog that had come into the vet under such horrible circumstances was looking for her forever home, and Bianca was honestly shocked she hadn't thought of it first.

"Gem," Bianca called. The dog immediately gave Luna and Ella one last affectionate lick before coming to Bianca's side and sitting. "Good girl." Bianca gave Gem an ear rub and slipped her a treat.

Gem was perfect—playful yet responsive to training, seemed to be some blend of Labrador retriever and a boxer, and loved to go on long runs with Maeve every day.

Bianca caught Maeve's stare from where she stood at the altar, her breath catching.

That was another thing that felt a little perfect; Maeve had moved in this past summer. Bianca loved waking up with her every morning. Then they'd pointlessly arguing with one another about who Gem loved best, do all the mundane things that Bianca had been dreaming about, and then she'd fall a little more in love when Maeve would roll over on top of her and kiss her like they were going off to war instead of their respective jobs.

"Love you," Bianca mouthed silently.

"Love you more," Maeve mouthed back.

And really, that was all Bianca wanted. To spend the rest of her life trying to out love the woman of her dreams.

* * *

Maeve didn't consider herself an especially emotional person—at least, she hadn't a year ago. Now, she was holding back tears as Sawyer and Quinn recited their vows. Maybe because she was starting to understand a love like theirs, now that she'd found her own.

Gem and Bianca had done a perfect job with the rings, and she snuck glances at them, seated on the far end of the first row. Bianca looked beautiful in a cut-out maxi dress that made her eyes look impossibly green. Seeing Bianca in it had set them back more than a few minutes earlier today, but that had been time-well used as far as Maeve was concerned.

She didn't know if she'd ever get used to the wanting. To be close. To be the person Bianca depended on. To want to prove to both of them that she was the woman Bianca seemed to see when she looked at her.

Maeve was able to focus on Sawyer and Bianca until Quinn started her vows and said, "I've loved you for twenty years now. Across time and distance and all the obstacles in between. Loving you for the rest of them, and getting to finally be with you while I do it, feels like the easy part."

Maeve's focus shifted back to Bianca, who looked like romanticism personified, hands clasped to her chest as she held onto Gem's leash.

The ring in Maeve's pocket felt like it was going to float out at any moment. With Sawyer and Quinn's blessing already, after the ceremony, she was going to slip away with Bianca to a small garden where Christmas lights had been strung around the trellis at the entryway.

That was where Maeve was going to propose, and to try and give Bianca even half of what she deserved in this world—including Maeve, if she wanted to have her.

Soon after things had become official, they'd started talking in generalities that had quickly become concrete. Living arrangements and vacations and job decisions had become things they discussed together as a team. Bianca hadn't seriously brought up marriage, but Maeve knew that was only because Bianca was trying to let her set the pace. Even if the idea of something this serious was newer to Maeve, it didn't make her want it any less than Bianca.

If anything, she was having all of these ideas and wants and hopes for the first time, and she was still struck with the intensity at which they washed over her. Feeling this level of love and affection and the simple, heady rush of knowing that they'd picked one another to be each other's *person* was exhilarating.

In about an hour, she'd tell Bianca all of those things.

Whatever Maeve had thought she was doing with her life, it hadn't really started until she'd met Bianca Rossi—who'd shown her that untangling the strands of Christmas lights was worth every ounce of struggle and effort. Except, she hadn't realized that the reason she'd done it wasn't the tree that lit up in a dizzying array of beautiful colors—it was so that she could.

And she never wanted that brightness to fade.

THE END

About the Author

Monica McCallan was an enthusiastic fan of romance novels before she began writing them. She currently lives in Philadelphia after a decade spent in the Bay Area, working at startups which gives her lots of great inspiration for the settings and storylines of her contemporary romance novels.

She posts about her dog on Twitter way too much, cannot parallel park to save her life, plays pool a few times a week, and has enjoyed every second of the craft beer explosion these last few years.

You can follow her on Twitter @monicamccallan

A Quick Note

Thank you for purchasing my book! If you'd like to stay updated on future releases, you can visit my website to sign up for my mailing list.

As an independent author, reviews on Amazon and Goodreads are greatly appreciated!

For any questions or inquiries, please email monica.mccallan@gmail.com